VALENTINED

(An Essie Cobb Senior Sleuth Mystery)

by

Patricia Rockwell

For information, email **Cozy Cat Press**, cozycatpress@aol.com or visit our website at: www.cozycatpress.com

COZY CAT
P R E S S

ISBN: 978-0-9848402-6-7
Printed in the United States of America

Cover design by Atomic Werewolf Studio
www.atomicwerewolfstudio.com

10 9 8 7 6 5 4 3 2 1

Dedicated to Milt, my own dear valentine

Chapter One

"When love is in excess it brings a man no honor nor worthiness."

—Euripides

Essie peered through the tiny window in her mailbox. She could see a hand holding a large, thick envelope heading directly towards her face. She pulled back as Phyllis, the front desk clerk at Happy Haven, squeezed the large-sized envelope carefully into her small cubicle. Essie waited patiently as Phyllis added several additional items—probably flyers for cemetery plots, which Essie received regularly in her mail by the bucketful. Not unusual for a ninety-year-old woman. She tapped her fingers on her walker handle bars as Phyllis continued to attempt to squeeze all of Essie's mail into the small compartment. While she waited for Phyllis to finish her delivery duties, Essie glanced above the wall of mailboxes—probably at least a hundred or more of the little bronze squares—one for each resident at the Happy Haven Assisted Living Facility. Hanging above the wall of boxes was a dangling banner of sparkly red and pink cardboard hearts. Valentine's Day was just a few days away and Happy Haven always went all out to decorate for each holiday. On the wall beside the mailboxes, a large poster advertised the facility's big upcoming Valentine's Day event—a speaker referred to on the ad as "Dr. Love—Guru of Valentine's Day and its History." *Just what a bunch of old people need,* Essie thought, *lectures in love.*

She looked back at her mailbox door. Phyllis had finished squeezing Essie's mail into her box and had moved on to another resident's box. Essie reached out and carefully twisted her box's combination lock to the correct code, opened the little door, and removed the pile of mail which included the large, thick envelope she had noticed Phyllis jamming in a few seconds ago. *Probably some cheesy card from one of my children,* she thought. *Kurt, no doubt,* she guessed. Of her three offspring, Kurt was the only boy and the only one who didn't live nearby. He tended to send her more elaborate cards on holidays than her two girls— Claudia and Prudence—who were more likely to bring her something in person. Of course, Essie didn't need cards from her children to feel appreciated, but it obviously gave them some pleasure to do these little things for her. Truthfully, she didn't need anything. She had enough *things*. She glanced down at her handful of mail. More than usual. Typically, she'd wait until she returned to her small apartment to go through it all, but the large envelope was beckoning to her and she wanted to see what kind of card Kurt had selected. It was really big. Maybe her son was feeling guilty because he hadn't visited in quite a while. She hoped that wasn't the case. She knew it was difficult for him to come to see her as regularly as her girls did.

Essie rolled her trusty red and black walker down the mailbox hallway and into the Happy Haven front lobby. On this cold February day, the fireplace in the lobby was lit and a crackling fire filled the large room with warmth. Large red cardboard hearts were placed strategically on the walls and a life-sized plastic Cupid that was supposed to appear to be marble graced the front entrance—the frozen archer boy apparently ready to shoot everyone entering with one of his trusty, love-drenched arrows. Essie maneuvered her vehicle over to a stuffed chair directly in front of the fire and plopped herself down. She placed the pieces of mail on her lap. There were so many items that they formed a large pile. Phyllis had exited from the tiny hallway behind the wall of mailboxes and had returned to her regular post behind the front desk on the other side of the lobby. Residents and staff moved across the lobby. Some were seated near Essie, apparently enjoying the fire too.

"Good morning, Essie," said a rotund man on a nearby sofa. His soft voice was barely audible, but Essie recognized it and she turned in her seat to face him.

"Good morning, Hubert," she replied. "Doesn't this fire feel good?"

"It does," the man said, nervously fingering his red suspenders and glancing down.

"Red suspenders for Valentine's Day, Hubert?" she asked.

"Yes," he said, glancing up shyly. "It's my favorite holiday, Miss Essie."

"Really?" she asked with a smile. "Why is that?"

"Because," he said, "because...well...I don't really know, Miss Essie. But I really like Valentine's Day."

"I do too," agreed Essie with a broad smile and a pat on Hubert's knee. The slight touch she gave him obviously was more than the man was expecting and he giggled and pulled—no, snapped—his suspenders in response. With a grin, Essie pulled back from Hubert. She knew he had a serious crush on her and she didn't want to encourage him too much. For her, Hubert Darby was a friend—a sweet friend—but certainly there was no romantic future there, at least for her. Her great love had been her late husband John. There wouldn't be another.

She thumbed through her mail, ignoring the obvious bills and advertisements. Selecting the large envelope, she read the front. Yes, it was addressed to her—Essie Cobb at Happy Haven Assisted Living Facility, with the correct street address in Reardon. But, the return address wasn't one she recognized. It certainly wasn't Kurt's address in a nearby state, which she knew by heart. She peered intently at the squiggly handwriting in the upper left-hand corner. She couldn't quite make out the numbers or the name of the street, but it appeared that the state was Massachusetts. Boston, in fact. *Hmm.* As she glanced to the right of the address, she noticed the stamp on the envelope. It had been postmarked yesterday in Boston, Massachusetts. *How strange*, she thought. *I don't know anyone in Boston.*

Santos, her favorite waiter from the dining room, walked purposely across the lobby bearing a food tray. He headed down her hallway to the far right of the family room. Essie realized that he was probably taking a meal to a resident in her wing. She tried to think what person in her wing might be ill or incapacitated enough to require a meal to be delivered, but she couldn't think of anyone. She'd have to ask Santos at lunch who it was who was getting the tray.

Phyllis was now speaking with Violet Hendrickson, Happy Haven's administrator, who had just come out of her office near the front entrance. The two women were talking in an animated fashion at the front desk. Essie always stayed far away from Violet because she had had more than her share of run-ins with the authoritarian woman. Violet ran a tight ship at Happy Haven and Essie had a tendency to circumvent rules when they didn't suit her. She and Violet had butted heads a number of times in the past and Essie had learned that it was probably best to just avoid the stern director. So she did just that. Turning her body away from the front desk, she faced the fireplace more directly, and refocused her attention on the elegant envelope resting on her lap.

Normally if she were in her room, she would use her plastic letter opener to nudge the flap up on the envelope. But as she didn't have this device with her at the moment, she resorted to using her not very sharp fingernails to scrape open the back of the envelope a bit until she was able to grab a larger portion of the flap and pull it up and away from the back of the envelope. Her curiosity was really getting to her now. She knew that she didn't know anyone in Boston. Who would be sending her a card from there? She reached into the envelope and tugged at the card inside. The fit was snug but Essie carefully removed the thick card from its container and then turned it over to view it from the front.

What she saw amazed her. It was definitely a valentine. The card was extremely elaborate—complete with a doily, ribbons, and a large, pink, three-dimensional silk heart placed right in the center. Gold lettering declared, "Happy Valentine's Day to My Beloved." *What?* thought Essie. *This is not a card from a friend or relative.* She quickly opened the card and read the gushy sentimental poem inside.

Fairly standard drivel, she concluded. Then the signature. She expected this little mystery to be solved as soon as she saw who had sent this masterpiece of mush, but the card was signed "Your Secret Admirer." *What? I don't know anyone in Boston*, she argued with herself. *How could I have a secret admirer there?*

Phyllis and Violet were continuing their discussion at the front desk. In fact, it was becoming more heated. Phyllis came out from behind the desk and headed towards the mailboxes. Violet followed her close behind. The two women appeared oblivious to Essie and the few other residents who were sitting in the lobby. As they passed, Violet glanced over and noticed Essie and the other residents ensconced in front of the fireplace. She stopped abruptly; leaving Phyllis stranded in the middle of the hallway, clearly uncertain whether to continue on or to wait for Violet. Violet moved slowly and purposefully over to the residents by the fireplace, smiling warmly at them.

"Good morning, everyone," she said to the few people gathered around the fireplace. "I see you're all enjoying the warmth of the fire on this cold day." Some of the residents mumbled a response, but most—including Essie—were dumbstruck that their illustrious leader had deigned to make an appearance in the lobby, let alone speak to any of them. They were far more used to having her spend her days in her office and allow her surrogates such as Phyllis and Sue Barber, the activities director, do all of the interacting with residents. Of course, Essie had had a few direct interactions with Violet Hendrickson and none of them had been pleasant. Violet was quite capable of making the Happy Haven residents feel more like misbehaving teenagers than responsible adults.

Violet looked around at the residents sitting in front of the fireplace. Her eyes focused on Essie. Essie cringed, although there was no reason for her to feel guilty—at least, this time. She wasn't doing anything wrong. *Oh, horrors of Henry!* she cried to herself. *Why does this woman always make me feel like a criminal? Stop this, Essie! You live here. Happy Haven is your home.*

"Good morning, Miss Hendrickson," she said to Violet, giving her a big, cheesy smile and fluttering her sparse eyelashes.

"Good morning, Essie," replied Violet. She stood tall, her beautiful posture enhanced by the trim blue designer suit she wore. She tapped her long, elegantly polished fingernails along the edge of her ever present clipboard. Phyllis edged in closer behind her.

"Miss Hendrickson," whispered Phyllis in Violet's ear, "you wanted to check on that—problem—in the back."

Violet continued staring at Essie—ignoring Phyllis—as Essie and the other residents returned her glare with frozen, smiling faces. Suddenly, Violet broke her eyes away from Essie, turned abruptly, and headed out the back with Phyllis following rapidly behind her. Essie looked around at the other residents sitting in front of the fireplace and shrugged. The residents scowled and returned to their reverie. One woman said, "She's a strange bird." Hubert Darby nodded and sighed. Essie couldn't have agreed more.

Her opinion of Violet Hendrickson did not weigh on her mind for long, however. She was soon drawn back into contemplation about the elegant, romantic valentine that rested on her lap. She had a secret admirer. In Boston, no less! *Now who would be sending me a valentine all the way from across the country? So beautiful! And in secret!* She picked up the card and turned it over and over, examining it. She glanced over at Hubert who still had his head down. She knew he would be able and willing to send her a valentine—maybe even one he'd signed as a secret admirer. But she couldn't imagine how he'd manage to have it sent from Boston. She didn't see Hubert as that clever or designing. Indeed, as she looked over at him, he seemed oblivious of the card she was reading and more just shy in her presence—which was the way he always seemed.

No, she reasoned. *There is another story to this card. A secret admirer. Hmm. Who could it be? Who would have a crush on a ninety-year-old widow in an assisted living facility? Like me?*

Chapter Two

"The first duty of love is to listen."

—Paul Tillich

Much later, she was still sitting in the lobby staring at the beautiful valentine when she looked up and realized that the residents in the first lunch seating were lining up at the dining hall door waiting to be allowed to enter. She was in the group of residents who ate their meals first. She could see her tablemates already in line, so she gathered her belongings, placed her mail and her secret admirer valentine in the little basket directly beneath the seat of her walker, and headed over to join them. Just as she arrived, Santos opened the doors to the dining hall and the residents began pouring into the large room. Essie often thought that sometimes the residents (and she included herself) acted like school children waiting to get into a circus rather than mature adults simply waiting for their dinners. For many residents, however, meals were the highlight of their days at Happy Haven. It was the time when they got out of their rooms and had a chance to socialize with other residents. A chance to find out what was happening in their little community. *A chance to gossip,* Essie admitted to herself. She pushed her walker through the dining hall entrance and towards her table.

When she arrived at her assigned table in the approximate center of the large dining hall, she saw that her three friends were already seated. She scooted her walker into position beside her chair, just as her tablemates had parked theirs. The only exception was Fay on the far side of the table who used a motorized wheelchair. One of the kitchen workers always made sure that the chair in Fay's place was removed so Fay could drive her power vehicle directly to her spot at the table. Essie parked her walker abruptly, slammed on the handbrake, and eased into her chair.

"Essie," said the tall, grey-haired woman to her right, "you're late! So unlike you."

"Yes," agreed the lively brunette to her left, "you're usually here before us! Always so impatient to eat!"

"Oh, jiggle jingles, Marjorie!" replied Essie to her critical friend. "I'm no more interested in eating than anyone else." And, of course, she realized that most residents were very interested in eating.

"Maybe not," said the other woman, "but you usually are here first!"

"I like to be on time, Opal," replied Essie to her other companion. "It's just one of my habits."

"So," said Marjorie with curiosity, "why are you late today? I think I saw you talking to Hubert Darby out in the lobby when I got in line. Don't tell me he's romancing you again?"

"It is closing in on Valentine's Day," noted Opal to Marjorie. "Hubert is notoriously romantic. And we all know what a crush he has on Essie... ."

"Stop it, Opal," interjected Essie. "Hubert and I were just making polite conversation."

"That's where it starts," said Marjorie with a sly shake of her shoulders. Her sparkling brown curls belied her age which was only evidenced by her facial wrinkles. *Marjorie is obviously enjoying this*, thought Essie. Whenever Marjorie puffed out her sweater as she was doing now, Essie knew that Marjorie was no doubt reliving some of her past youthful follies.

"Not every conversation between a man and a woman is destined to lead to romance, Marjorie," said Essie with finality.

"Maybe not for you," agreed Marjorie, "but I view such conversations as rife with possibilities." She flipped her hands in the air, tossing her curls up in the process. Essie huffed.

"We can probably present this situation to our upcoming guest speaker," observed Opal, maintaining her distance. Unlike Marjorie, Opal never had a hair out of place on her neatly coifed grey head. She was always well groomed and totally inconspicuous, just as she had been in her career as an administrative assistant to one of the top lawyers in Reardon.

"Guest speaker?" asked Essie, happy to change the subject.

"Yes," said Opal, nodding. "You may have noticed the signs. Some gentleman named 'Dr. Love.'" Opal raised her eyebrows dramatically. "It appears that he's an anthropologist who has studied the history of romantic love. He's scheduled to speak here in a few days."

"Oh, yes!" said an excited Marjorie. "On Valentine's Day! How appropriate!"

"Boiled bodkins," said Essie. "Not something that interests me in the slightest. Or apparently Fay either." She glanced across the table at the fourth member of the group who had nodded off in her wheelchair. "Was it something we said, Fay?" When her name was mentioned, the plump little lady awakened abruptly and gave a puzzled smile to all three of her tablemates.

At that point, Santos arrived at the table with his pad. The ladies quickly picked up the menus placed on their plates and glanced down at the few entree selections for the luncheon meal.

"Ladies need more time to make decision?" he asked. "Santos can return." He started to turn, but Essie grabbed his jacket.

"No, Santos," she said to the young Hispanic waiter, "we're ready. Aren't we, ladies?"

As each woman rattled off her choice of items from the menu, Santos busily jotted down their preferences on his pad. When he finished, he turned to leave.

"Santos," said Essie, pulling him back. "I saw you headed down my hallway this morning with a food tray. Is someone sick down there? I think I know everyone in my hall and I wasn't aware that anyone there was ill." She smiled sweetly, waiting for Santos to respond.

"Not sure, Miss Essie," he said, furrowing his brow and biting his lower lip. "Can't remember. I take meals to so many residents. Sorry." With that, he turned away and retreated into the kitchen.

"How strange!" said Essie. "I can't believe Santos wouldn't remember whom he delivered breakfast to so quickly. He's usually so sharp."

"Maybe he doesn't want to tell you, Essie," said Marjorie, poking her finger into Essie's shoulder. "You are a bit of a busybody."

"Me!" replied Essie. "If anyone should win an award for gossip-monger of the year, Marjorie, it should be..."

"Stop it, you two!" cried Opal, gesturing firmly for her friends to cease their bickering. Fay mumbled in her sleep, raising an eyelid at the increased noise level. "See," continued Opal, "you woke Fay up!"

Fay shook herself and looked around. She peered down at her empty plate, and seeing that it contained no food, she slowly drifted off to sleep again.

"That's neither here nor there," continued Essie.

"It's actually here, Essie," snapped Marjorie. "Fay is at our table. She is about as 'here' as anyone can get, besides the three of us."

"You know what I mean, Marjorie! Anyway, that's not what I wanted to tell you all. I actually have something I want to show you."

"Show us?" asked Opal with a deep intake of breath. She peered down her long, aquiline nose at Essie, then quickly over at Marjorie, almost as if daring her to interrupt.

"Yes," replied Essie, as Marjorie pouted with her trademark shoulder shake. "I received a valentine in the mail this morning."

"Oh, how nice!" exclaimed Opal. "From one of your children?"

"I wish," said Essie, scowling. Her shoulders slumped and she stared at her plate in renewed contemplation of her dilemma. Should she show the card to her friends? She knew that the minute they saw it, they'd begin to imagine some major romantic tryst between her and this unknown gentleman. On the other hand, without their input it would be unlikely that she'd ever figure out who had sent the card. Truly, her three friends had helped her solve other mysteries in the past and she had faith that their assistance would be key in deciphering this one. She leaned over to the seat on her walker and lifted it. Reaching inside, she drew out the large envelope on top.

"I got this in the mail this morning," she announced. She removed the valentine from the envelope and handed it to Opal.

"My goodness, Essie," said Opal, "this is a beautiful valentine. I've never seen such an elaborate card!"

"That's what I thought," agreed Essie.

"Let me see it!" demanded Marjorie, reaching across the table in an attempt to grab the card from Opal.

"Wait a minute," said Opal, shoving away Marjorie's hands as she opened the card. "It's signed 'your secret admirer.'"

"I know," said Essie.

"You have a secret admirer, Essie!" exclaimed Marjorie. "I want to see it!" She reached for the card again, and this time Opal allowed her tablemate to have the card. Marjorie examined the card, both outside and inside, ooing and awing at all of its parts.

"Who do you think sent it, Essie?" asked Opal.

"I wish I knew," responded Essie.

"Hubert?" blurted Marjorie.

"No," said Essie. "It can't be him."

"Why not?" asked Opal. "You know he has a crush on you."

"There must be other men here at Happy Haven, Essie," noted Marjorie, "that like you. Any one of them could have sent this to you." She continued to stare at the card, touching it almost reverently.

"It isn't anyone at Happy Haven," Essie said emphatically. "In fact, it isn't anyone in Reardon." She turned over the envelope on her plate and handed it to Opal. "Check out the return address and the postmark."

"Boston, Massachusetts," Opal read from the envelope.

"Right," said Essie.

"Who do you know in Boston?" asked Marjorie, her eyes flashing with excitement.

"No one," replied Essie, slapping her palms firmly on the table. "That's the mystery. No one. I don't know a soul in Boston. So who could have sent this to me?"

"Now, Essie," said Opal, grabbing the envelope from Marjorie, and then examining it as if it were one of the crown jewels. "You probably do know who this person is; you've just forgotten that you know him."

"Right!" agreed Marjorie. "Maybe it's an old college beau! He's loved you for years and now is just making contact with you after all these years because...because...I know! His wife just died and he wants to get back together with you!" She clasped her hands together and almost swayed as if to some romantic tune that only she could hear.

"So why didn't he sign his name?" asked Essie.

At that moment, Santos returned to their table with their four meals balanced expertly in his outstretched arms. He carefully placed each at the appropriate place and then turned to go. Just then, he glanced down and saw the elegant, flowery valentine in the center of the table.

"What beautiful valentine!" he cried. "For you, Miss Essie?"

"It's from her secret admirer!" said Marjorie.

"Marjorie!" Essie scolded. "That was supposed to be a secret."

"No worry, Miss Essie," said Santos. "Santos can keep secret. I no tell anyone you have secret admirer."

"I know you won't, Santos," said Essie, looking pointedly into his eyes. "You're quite good at keeping secrets."

The young man blushed and mumbled something about the kitchen and then he quickly headed out.

"You shouldn't have mentioned this to Santos, Marjorie!" said Essie.

"Oh, Essie," Marjorie replied flippantly. "He won't say anything. He probably won't even remember he heard about it."

"Even so," said Essie. "I'd like to keep this quiet."

"We understand, Essie," agreed Opal. She nodded politely to Essie while giving Marjorie one of her stern looks.

"Personally," said Marjorie, ignoring Opal. "If I had a secret admirer—no matter where he lived—I'd shout it to the world!"

Chapter Three

"There is always some madness in love. But there is also always some reason in madness."

—Friedrich Nietzsche

Essie had returned to her apartment. She was no wiser about the identity of her secret admirer, even though her friends all had numerous ideas—most of them frivolous—about who the person might be. She was peeved. As she rolled into her small living room, she headed immediately for her tiny bathroom where she performed her post-meal ritual of potty, purifying, and primping. That is, she first relieved her bladder which was always full and seemed to require constant attention. Her daughters were forever after her to wear those disgusting adult diapers, but Essie had too much pride, and as long as she could move, she would go to the bathroom on her own. After this, she always washed her hands religiously with the hottest water possible to prevent the spread of germs. Her purifying routine. Then, finally, after the necessities were complete, she indulged in a few minutes of face-fixing. That meant a bit of hair fluffing, cheek squeezing, and maybe the addition of a bit of lipstick. That was all she ever indulged in. Of course, she knew many women at Happy Haven who did much more to maintain—rather enhance—their appearance, but Essie was not particularly vain and she firmly believed that her best feature was her gleaming smile which she exhibited freely to almost everyone. Indeed, her late husband John had never seemed to be upset with her minimal use of make-up and that was all that mattered to Essie.

She looked in the tiny mirror in her bathroom and squeezed her cheeks with her fingertips. A rosy glow quickly bloomed on her face. *Not so bad*, she thought. A friendly face with nice brown eyes encircled in her glasses and also by a ring of sparkling, snow white curls. She moved her lips around, puckering them, frowning, giving the mirror various types of smiles. *You have a secret admirer*, she said to herself in the glass. She tipped her head to the side flirtatiously, pulling off her glasses seductively. *Oh, bungling burglars, Essie Cobb! You sound like some teenage school girl! Are you going to let a silly greeting card get you in a tizzy like this?* She grimaced at her blurry reflection, the image seeming to provide her answer. She shoved her glasses back on over her ears and headed her walker out of her bathroom and into her little main room.

Essie rolled her walker over to her favorite armchair, a big paisley recliner. She slid easily into the soft cushion, leaving her walker nearby. Placing the footrest up, she was now in her favorite spot. From here she could reach anything on her desk with her right hand and anything on her end table with her left hand. Pulling her walker closer, she lifted the lid of the seat and pulled out the secret admirer card. She leaned back and began to contemplate the mysterious piece of mail. For many minutes, she just stared at the envelope. Then, she removed the card inside and did the same for the greeting card, staring at it for a long time. She tried to describe the envelope and the card to herself.

First, the envelope. *As greeting card envelopes go*, she thought, *this one is fairly distinctive*. The envelope was not plain white like most envelopes; it was a cream, or more a yellowish color. The paper was not the typical typewriter paper quality envelope that most of her bills came in. The paper that this envelope was made from was thick; she could see the weave in it almost as it it were closer to being cloth than paper. *Very beautiful*. Not only that, the inside of the envelope was lined with a gold foil, providing an extra layer of protection for the card inside. Essie thought that given how elaborate the card itself was, it was probably a good idea that the envelope was designed to be comparable in quality to the card. She also examined the back flap of the envelope. It was a typical gummed closing. She couldn't tell if the sender had actually licked the envelope or moistened it with a sponge or some other device. *Not that that is an important detail*, she thought. Or maybe it was. Maybe her secret admirer was not only an over-the-top romantic, but maybe he was also a germaphobe and didn't want to get his bacteria on the envelope that he was mailing to his beloved. *Ridiculous, Essie!* she thought. *Now that is a flight of fancy.*

Next, she lifted out the card again for a more thorough examination. She realized the difficulty in extracting the card from the envelope. It wasn't because the sender had included any additional items in the card. It was merely because there was so much decoration on the front of it. All of the doilies, ribbons, embossed lettering, and most important, the raised silk heart in the center made the card very thick. It took effort to remove it from the envelope. It took even more effort to replace it inside the envelope.

Essie held the card gingerly in her hands. She stared at the front of it, delighting in its beauty. The design was simple but elegant. A large white doily formed the base and was attached (she determined by carefully pulling up an edge)

with glue on the front of the card. Winding in and out
around the edge of the doily was a thin, pink, silk ribbon.
She realized that the effort required to accomplish just this
portion of the card, the weaving of the ribbon into the doily,
must have taken a huge amount of time—far more time
than most greeting card companies would allot to such
efforts. Surely, this aspect of the card alone made it an
extremely expensive one. *Expensive*, she thought. *Just
how much would such a card cost these days?* She mused
about the last time she could remember buying a greeting
card. She had a sack full of greeting cards that she kept in
the lower left-hand corner of her desk that she used when
she had to send birthday cards to her grandchildren or get
well cards to friends at Happy Haven. But Claudia had
bought all of these cards for her long ago. She never asked
her youngest daughter how much she'd spent on these
simple greeting cards. In her day, Essie remembered that
the few times she ever purchased a greeting card, it cost
her maybe 50 cents or so. That was probably not the case
today, and certainly was probably not the case with this
card. This card was probably very expensive—maybe
several dollars. Maybe even ten!

She put the doily back down, not wanting to rip it. Like
most doilies, this one was paper-thin and very delicate.
Essie put her finger on the gold letters on the front of the
card. They were raised—embossed. The gold sparkled and
shone. It didn't look like it had just been printed by a
printing press. It looked specially applied with just these
unique letters for this particular card. She ran her finger
over the smooth letters. They felt slightly rough to the
touch—unlike the feel of the surrounding paper.

She next focused her attention on the beautiful silk heart in the center of the doily. This heart was obviously made out of a silk-looking cloth. Maybe it was real silk. It was three-dimensional. That is, it looked like a stuffed teddy bear, only it was a stuffed heart. Essie touched it gently and there was a slight give to the heart. There was obviously some stuffing inside. *Maybe cotton or whatever they put in stuffed animals,* she reasoned. She carefully pulled at the edge of the heart, peeking underneath to see how it was attached. This endeavor was not as easy as her attempt to peek under the doily. The heart was firmly anchored to the doily beneath it. Apparently, its base was glued to the doily at all points. *Strange,* thought Essie. She continued gently pulling at the heart all around its edges to see if she could see any part of the perimeter that was not tightly attached to the doily beneath. There was no break. The heart would not give.

Admitting defeat in this aspect of her greeting card investigation, Essie turned to the inside of the card. She re-read the poem printed on the inside page. The text of the poem seemed to her to be incredibly gushy, romantic drivel. She couldn't imagine anyone—even her own husband—actually sending such sentimental claptrap with a straight face to anyone they actually cared for. This observation caused her to reflect on the many cards she had received from her late husband. He had definitely sent her cards for many different events—birthdays, anniversaries, holidays, and even some spontaneous moments in their life together. Never, however, did he—or would he—send her anything as mushy as this poem. Most of John's cards to her, Essie recalled, were personal and—yes—funny! He knew she liked humor and so did he! Most of the cards she gave John

were funny too. *We were just not a very romantic couple*,
she concluded. She knew that didn't mean they didn't love
each other. It just meant that they were not as overtly
demonstrative as...as...this cloying, almost creepy card from
her secret admirer.

Yes, the secret admirer. Essie glanced down at the
signature. She stared at the handwriting. She tried to think
if she remembered it from anywhere or anyone. It didn't
look familiar. The handwriting was simple. It was written
in blue ink. That is, it had not been printed by machine. A
real person somewhere (in Boston?) had actually signed this
card and sent it intentionally to her—Essie Cobb. Now how
could she figure out who this person was? Was it man?
Woman? Child? She had no idea.

She was becoming disgusted at having to deal with this
problem. Annoyed, she flipped the card over and looked at
the back. The only marking on the fourth and final page of
the valentine was a logo declaring "Boston Bell Greeting
Cards" in the center of the page. A black and white drawing
of what appeared to be the cracked Liberty Bell sat on the
left side of the logo, tipped at a jaunty angle. On the right,
the letters indicating the company name were shown in a
dramatic dark font that gave the entire logo an early
American feel. *I guess that's appropriate*, noted Essie. It
did come from Boston. Then she remembered that the
Liberty Bell was actually at Independence Hall in
Philadelphia—not Boston. Was that a clue? Was the card
actually produced in Philadelphia? *And besides*, thought
Essie, *who cares where my secret admirer purchased the
card or what company made it? What matters is who sent
it*. The back of the card looked strangely naked with just the

card company's small logo in the center. Essie pondered why the greeting card back page seemed so barren to her but she couldn't figure it out. Eventually, she picked up the card and stuffed it back in the fancy envelope and slipped it back in her walker basket.

I wish I knew more about this card and all of its features, she thought. The doily, the ribbon, the fancy cloth heart. Who would know about these features and how they were made? Essie thought and thought and finally it came to her. The answer was actually fairly nearby and—she looked over at the Happy Haven monthly activity calendar on her desk—fairly soon. She rose, stretched her arms, grabbed her walker, and headed out her door.

Chapter Four

"A woman has got to love a bad man or two in her life, to be thankful for a good one."

—Marjorie Kinnan Rawlings

Essie zoomed down her hallway, through the family room and into Happy Haven's only elevator which slowly managed to deposit her on the second and top floor. *I could probably climb the stairs, walker and all, faster than this dilapidated old can*, she thought. Scooting around a group of residents who were positioned to enter the elevator, Essie directed her walker down a hallway that veered off the small central lobby on the second floor. A few yards down this hallway, an open double door revealed a large room filled with tables. All of the tables were covered with various art supplies. In the center of the room, Sue Barber, the Happy Haven activities director, was busy encouraging residents in the construction of valentines. Essie entered the room and quietly found an empty place at a table near the doorway.

"What's better than a homemade valentine?" Sue was asking the group. "Nothing says love more than something you make yourself!" She held up various pieces of paper. "You'll notice that we have a wide variety of paper that you can use for the base of your card."

Essie slid onto the empty chair. There were three women already there, each of them diligently at work constructing a valentine. Essie thought she knew most of the residents, but these three were strangers to her.

"Hi," she said to the group. "I'm Essie."

"Donna Grimes," replied the woman to her right. "I'm making a card for my husband."

"She doesn't have a husband," added the lady directly across from Essie and next to Donna. "She always makes him a card anyway."

"That's nice," replied Essie, not certain how to respond. Donna smiled sweetly, apparently oblivious to her friend's comment.

"I'm Velma. We're from C wing, second floor," added the woman.

"Nice to meet you," said Essie. "I'm Essie Cobb, C wing first floor." She smiled.

Sue Barber was describing various supplies that could be used to construct a valentine and how the residents might add their own individual touches to their creations. Donna and Velma were hard at work cutting, pasting, and folding.

Essie turned to the third woman at her table on her left who had so far remained speechless. "Hello, are you making a valentine too?" The woman smiled at Essie and held up a piece of red construction paper in response. *Hmmm*, thought Essie. *Just like Fay.*

Although she had no interest in actually making a valentine, Essie decided that she had best maintain a low profile, so she grabbed some of the items in the center of the table and began fashioning a valentine herself. Sue Barber continued to drone on from the center of the room, describing types of cards and various different things residents might do to create a truly beautiful valentine. Eventually, Sue ceased talking and announced that she would be coming around to each table to check to see how everyone was coming along with their creations. *Good,* thought Essie. *Now, maybe I can pick her brain about my secret admirer card.* She fiddled with some red and white construction paper, folding and molding it as she watched Sue make her way around the room, talking to each and every person at every table.

"Are you making a valentine for your husband too?" Donna asked Essie.

Essie was startled when her neighbor interrupted her train of thought. She glanced over at Donna, the lady who evidently believed her dead husband was still alive.

"No," she said cautiously. "I'm...I'm making this for..." Essie thought about her response, not wanting to aggravate Donna's grief by mentioning her own widowhood. She decided on a safe response. "Actually, I'm making this for my...new great grandson!" she proclaimed. Of course, Essie had no great grandchildren, and this lie was totally off the cuff. *Oh my!* she thought. *Now I've done it. I've told a lie to spare this woman's feelings. I'm sure I could have thought of something truthful to say that wouldn't have upset her.*

"That's so nice!" said Donna, smiling broadly.

"A great grandson," added Velma. "How wonderful!"

Essie smiled in acknowledgement, cowering inside. She glanced down at her red construction paper and grabbed a squeeze bottle of glue from the center of the table and lowered her head to her work, focusing like a laser beam on squeezing a small line of white glue all around the entire edge of her red paper. The other women returned to their valentine construction, and for several minutes everyone at the table was engrossed in their efforts.

As Essie continued her efforts to glue the entire perimeter of the large piece of red construction paper, she didn't notice Sue Barber moving to her table. Suddenly the young staff woman was there.

"And how are you ladies coming along with your masterpieces?" Sue asked with a breezy voice. She stood at the corner of the table between Donna and Essie. She focused on Donna's card—a pink heart pinned to three doilies. Essie noted that although Donna may have been confused about the state of her marriage, there was obviously no confusion about her artistic skills. She had fashioned something quite beautiful in the short time that Essie had been tediously gluing the edge of her construction paper.

"Oh, Donna!" exclaimed Sue, holding up the card in her hands. "This is beautiful!" Sue's face beamed a genuine smile. She tipped her head to the side in appreciation of Donna's workmanship. Sue's long, brown hair hung against her blue work smock. Essie noticed that, unlike their illustrious director Violet, Sue's fingertips were not beautifully trimmed and painted. In fact, Sue's hands and fingers looked like they spent a lot of time here in the recreation room working on art projects. She could see short nails, bitten down in spots, and hands that were rough and calloused. Essie glanced around the room where she could see displayed many art projects completed by residents. It was evident that Sue took pride in her efforts here and viewed each resident's artistic success as a personal triumph.

Sue continued to rave about Donna's card. "I love what you've done with the outlining here, Donna!" She pointed out to the women at the table the clever effect that Donna had created through the use of her doilies intertwined with her construction paper. "I can hardly wait to see this card completed!"

Sue placed the card back in Donna's hands. Donna was smiling proudly as Sue selected her work to highlight for the table. Sue then went to each person at the table and discussed their art work with them individually. She came to Essie last.

"Essie!" cried Sue. "We never see you here for our art classes!"

"Miss Barber," replied Essie. "Yes, I'm not much of an artist, really...."

"I can't believe that, Miss Essie," interjected Sue. "You are one of the cleverest residents at Happy Haven. I bet you'll make an amazing valentine."

"Oh, I doubt that," said Essie, embarrassed. "Actually, Miss Barber, I was wondering if I might ask you a question."

"Of course."

"I'd really like to pick your brain," she began.

"Pick away," said Sue, laughing. "What do you need to know?"

"It's about valentines," said Essie.

"Appropriate," Sue said and nodded. This turn in the conversation seemed to get the other women at the table to stop their artwork and look over at them.

"Yes," said Essie. "I received a valentine that I'd like your professional opinion about." Essie reached over to her walker and lifted the seat. She handed the envelope to Sue.

"Oh, my!" declared Sue as Essie placed the card in her hands. "What's this?"

"Just look at it," Essie encouraged, "and tell me everything you can about it."

Sue's face revealed her puzzlement. Even so, with a slight smile, she gently opened the envelope and carefully removed the card inside. By now, not only were the three women at Essie's table totally focused on what was happening, other residents at other tables had stopped their artistic endeavors and were watching Sue Barber open Essie's card.

Sue stared at the front of Essie's valentine. She carefully opened the card and perused the inside poem and signature. Then, she turned it over and read the back. She turned the card back to the front.

"This is quite a card, Essie!" she said with almost a whistle. "And a secret admirer! You are some lady!" As soon as Sue said the words 'secret admirer' all the women at Essie's table gasped. Donna and Velma repeated the phrase and soon the words 'secret admirer' echoed throughout the rec room.

"No, no!" said Essie to Sue, "what I need to know is what can you tell me about the construction of this card? How was it manufactured? You're the resident art expert here and I was hoping you might enlighten me about the card itself. Anything you can tell me I would appreciate."

"Why, Essie, if you don't mind my asking, why do you need to know about how the card was created or manufactured? I would just be thrilled to get such a beautiful card—and from a secret admirer. Do you have any idea who it is?" Sue beamed with excitement.

"No," said Essie, "and I thought maybe you could help me figure out who it is if you could tell me something— anything—about the card itself."

"Oh, I see," said Sue with a nod. She looked around at the other women at the table. They were waiting for her response—as were apparently many others in the rec room—with baited breath. "I guess I'd better come up with something then." She laughed and smiled at Essie and the other women, and returned to her intense perusal of the card.

"Essie has a secret admirer!" called a man from a nearby table. Essie scowled at him. Her response was greeted with a few cat calls from several other men in the room, but they were quickly hushed by a chorus of women throughout the rec room who piped in about how romantic it was.

"I don't really know, Essie," said Sue finally. "There's not a lot to tell you about this card. It's well made, beautifully made, actually. In fact, I'd say the workmanship is far more precise than your typical store-bought greeting card. Most cards these days are mass-produced and don't have so much detail to them. I mean, just the front. Look at the doily and the delicate ribbon that is woven around the edge. That would take a lot of effort. Also, the stuffed heart in the center. You just don't see cards with little sachets like that anymore."

"Do you mean, Miss Barber," asked Essie, "that this card is an old card that someone just happened to have lying around and sent me?"

"I don't know, Essie," said Sue. "That's possible. They did make fancy cards like this years ago when people put more stock in sending really beautiful valentines. I remember my grandmother received a similar valentine from my grandfather once. She kept it for years. It had a little heart like this one too. It was actually a sachet that could be removed and used to perfume drawers where you kept sweaters. I remember my grandmother told me she had taken off the little heart and kept it in her intimates drawer—that's what she called her underwear drawer—for many years."

"Do you think the heart on this card is one of those sachets?" asked Essie.

"I don't know," said Sue. She held the front of the card up to her nose and sniffed. "It doesn't smell like it has any perfume or talcum powder in it, so I'd guess not. You can try to remove it and use it in a drawer if you like though."

"Oh, I don't think I'll do that," said Essie with a sigh. "I really just want to know who sent it to me. It's a mystery...and..."

"And Essie likes mysteries!" called out the gentleman who had earlier made the crack about Essie's secret admirer. Sue looked over at the man and gave him an admonishing glare and he quickly resumed work on his card.

"I guess that's all I can offer you, Essie," said Sue with finality as she handed the card back. "It is a curious situation. If you don't know who this person is, I don't know how you can find out who he is just by finding out more about the card. I wish you could. And I wish I could help you."

"That's okay, Miss Barber," replied Essie. "You've actually been very helpful." Essie said good-bye to her table companions and headed back to her apartment.

Chapter Five

"To love is to receive a glimpse of heaven"

—Karen Sunde

Back in her room, Essie was sitting in her recliner mulling over the information she had acquired from Sue Barber at the arts and crafts class. Not much, she realized. Sue had been impressed with the workmanship of the card, but other than that and the fact that she thought the little heart might contain some sort of sachet, Essie hadn't learned much in her trip up to the second floor. As she stared at the card, she thought of someone else who might be able to provide her with some pertinent information about the greeting card.

Grabbing her telephone from the end table to her right, she tapped in the numbers for her oldest daughter, Prudence. Pru answered on the first ring, which was typical.

"Hello."

"Pru? It's your mother."

"Oh, Mom! Hi! Is something wrong?" Essie smiled to herself. It was so like her eldest to immediately assume the worst when receiving a phone call from her mother.

"I'd really like to speak with Mindy, dear, if she's there." Pru's adult daughter Mindy lived at home with her parents while attempting to jump-start her career. The economy had taken a toll on the young woman whose college degree in graphic design wasn't in great demand in Reardon.

"Mindy? Well, yes, she's here, Mom. She's getting ready for work. I'll get her." Work was a part-time job at a local boutique. Mindy created ads and brochures, and designed the small company's website. Essie had seen samples of her work and had been surprised and delighted by her granddaughter's talent.

After a few seconds, Mindy spoke.

"Hey, Grandma! What's up?"

"Mindy, dear," began Essie, "I have a little problem that I believe you might be able to help me with."

"Me? Sure, Grandma," replied Mindy with a small laugh. "I can't imagine that there's anything I could do that Mom couldn't though."

"Oh, yes, dear," said Essie. "This is a problem in graphic design."

"Really?" exclaimed Mindy. "What are you making, Grandma?"

"Oh, dear, I'm not making anything," explained Essie. "I have something here that I'd like you to take a look at and tell me what you can about how it was made...or designed."

"You mean like an advertisement?" asked Mindy, her curiosity obviously piqued.

"No, dear. This is a greeting card. A valentine to be exact."

"A valentine?" cried Mindy. "One you received?"

"Yes, as a matter of fact," said Essie. "There are some very unusual things about it. I'd really like you to take a look at it. Do you think you might be able to drop by Happy Haven and do that?"

"Sure, Grandma," said Mindy. "Tell you what, I'm almost ready to leave for work, but Happy Haven is right on my way. If I leave now, I can drop by your place in a few minutes and check out your mysterious card before I head off to work. How's that?"

"That would be wonderful, dear!"

"Okay, I'm out the door!"

Essie hung up the phone, totally gratified that she would not only get Mindy's expert opinion on the mysterious valentine, but also that she'd have a chance to speak with her quiet young granddaughter alone and away from the often overbearing force of her mother. Essie made a quick bathroom trip as a precaution. She didn't want to be interrupted during Mindy's visit with the need to visit her facilities.

True to her word, Mindy arrived, breathless, about fifteen minutes later. Pru and her husband didn't live all that far away—a fact that provided constant security to Essie. Mindy tapped lightly on Essie's front door and then stuck her head in.

"Grandma?" she called out quietly.

"Come in, dear," said Essie, now back in her recliner, the card in question on her lap.

Mindy entered. She quickly removed her winter hat and jacket and came over to Essie, sitting on the desk chair that she moved over beside Essie's recliner. Mindy was a slight young woman with delicate features and long, loose strawberry blonde hair. She had a gentle smile on her face.

"It's so good to see you, Mindy," said Essie warmly.

"You too, Grandma," replied Mindy, giving her grandmother a short kiss on the top of her head. "How are you doing?"

"Physically, just fine, my dear," replied Essie, "but mentally I'm stumped. I hope you can help."

"I'll sure try."

"Look here," said Essie, holding up the valentine, now out of its envelope. "I received this in the mail." With a puzzled look, Mindy took the card. She studied the front, then opened the card and read the inside. Finally, she turned the card over and looked at the back. "Our activities director, Sue Barber, looked at it and said it was extremely well made. She thought the little heart in the center might be a sachet. You know, with perfume inside."

"Hmm," said Mindy, furrowing her brow as she studied the card. "It's very fancy. And what's this about a secret admirer? I take it you don't know who sent it?"

"No, dear," said Essie, "I have no idea who sent it. The postmark says Boston and I can't think of anyone I know who lives there."

"It's very romantic, Grandma," said Mindy looking directly at Essie. "Wow! I mean...it's pretty neat to have some guy send you something like this at...I mean..."

"You mean at my age?" asked Essie. "Oh, it's all right, dear. I long ago gave up any aspirations of having men ply me with romantic missives." Mindy chuckled.

"I don't see why not, Grandma," she said. "You're a neat lady."

"Thank you, Mindy, but I've only given my heart to one man in my life and that was your grandfather."

"I understand, Grandma," said Mindy. "Grandpa John was a super guy. I can understand why you loved him. He was always really nice to me."

"He loved you a lot, my dear," said Essie warmly as the two women sat next to each other, their arms touching as they stared at the flowery card. "But, anyway, that's not why I asked you here. I asked you because I know how talented a designer you are. I hope you might be able to tell me something about this card—how it was made, constructed, where, anything about the materials used. Just anything you can. I'm trying to figure out who sent it to me and I believe that the more I know about the card itself the better chance I stand of figuring out something about the man who sent it."

"I don't know that I can tell you much, Grandma," said Mindy tentatively, "but there are some things that jump out at me when I first look at it."

"Like what?"

"First, it was definitely made by an artist, probably a professional graphic designer like myself. I can tell by the designer's use of font, placement, color—oh, just a number of elements that suggest it is professionally done. However, I don't think this professional designer created this valentine for the Boston Bell Greeting Card Company." Mindy turned the card over and read the name of the company from the back of the card.

"Why do you say that, dear?"

"Grandma," she said, "the logo for the company on the back of the card would seem to indicate that it was manufactured by this company. But, I don't think so. I think this designer made this card specifically to send to you and not to be sold in stores. Do you have any other greeting cards around here?" She turned back to the desk and glanced around.

"I do," said Essie. "Look under that pile of papers in the upper right hand corner. There are several greeting cards I got for Christmas that I just haven't thrown away. Is that what you mean?"

"Yes," said Mindy, fumbling around in the pile for one of the old Christmas cards. She found one and brought it out. Turning the card over, she showed Essie the back. "Look at this Christmas card. It was obviously purchased in a store. What do you see on the back?"

"I see a logo just like on the valentine," said Essie, pulling down her glasses and squinting at the markings on the back of the card. "Then there's this square full of lines. I don't see that on the valentine."

"That's the UPC...the bar code," said Mindy. "There's no bar code on your secret admirer valentine like there is on this Christmas card or on any other card you might receive that was purchased in a store. This bar code is on everything purchased in a store because it's what the clerk uses to determine how much to charge for the item when you buy it. See, your valentine doesn't have a bar code. That means that it wasn't purchased in a store. I would venture a guess that it was made and sent to you directly by the person who made it. Very unusual."

"You mean," said Essie, trying to understand, "the person who sent me the valentine is the same person who made my valentine."

"I don't know for sure," said Mindy with a shrug, "but I would say probably yes."

"But why?" Essie asked, mystified. "Who would do that? Why would someone make such a beautiful card, making it look like it was bought, and then send it to me? Especially someone who doesn't even sign their name?"

"It seems the card designer and sender doesn't want you to know who he is," offered Mindy.

"But why?" asked Essie, more to herself than her granddaughter. "Why go to all that effort for... nothing?"

"Maybe it wasn't for nothing," suggested Mindy.

"I don't see what the person who sent me this card gets by sending it," mused Essie.

"He knows you know he cares for you," said Mindy.

"But I don't know! I don't know who he is! Oh, I'm so confused!" cried Essie, throwing her hands up.

"Don't be upset, Grandma," said Mindy, reaching over and giving her grandmother a warm hug. "You have a secret admirer. Even if you don't know who he is, you know someone out there really likes you. Actually, Grandma, I'm jealous! I wish some guy felt so strongly about me that he'd send me something as beautiful as this! And so would Mom!"

"What?" asked Essie, turning back to her granddaughter, her thoughts now totally on Mindy. "What's this about your mother?"

"Oh, you know," said Mindy, looking down as if ashamed. "She's always hounding me about finding a guy and I'm just not very good at doing that."

"Your mother!" exclaimed Essie. "I should whip her little behind! She has no right to tell you how to run your love life. Oh, Mindy, I could tell you stories of Prudence and some of the boys she brought home when she was your age! Yikes and bikes! There was this one horrible fellow who always smelled like onions and looked like he slept in a garbage bin. Prudence was enamored of him for months before she discovered that he had lice. Then she dropped him like a hot potato. Hopefully, lice were all he had!"

"This was Mom's boyfriend?" asked a skeptical Mindy.

"Oh, yes, dear," said Essie, shaking her head. "I could tell you many stories about your mother's romantic escapades.

Would you like some additional stories to use in your future defense?"

"Oh, thanks, Grandma," replied Mindy, laughing, "but I think I can handle her. We just have two different viewpoints about the importance of men in my life right now."

"I hear you, dear," said Essie. "At the moment, given this mystifying secret admirer, I'm about ready to give up on the whole sex!"

"You go, Grandma!" said Mindy with an encouraging fist pump.

"Girl power!" added Essie with a matching hand gesture. The two women, generations apart, smiled and hugged again.

After offering her professional opinion in regards to all elements of the card, Mindy eventually gathered her belongings and headed off to work. Essie remained in her recliner, staring at her card, a bit wiser than she had been before her granddaughter's arrival—both about the card and about Mindy.

Chapter Six

"Love sought is good, but given unsought is better."

—Shakespeare

Later at dinner, Essie and her pals were continuing their analysis of the strange case of Essie's valentine and secret admirer while they savored their after dinner coffee.

"My granddaughter Mindy came over today and looked at the card," Essie explained to her tablemates. "She's a graphic designer."

"Have I met your granddaughter?" asked Opal.

"I don't know, Opal," said Essie. "If you did, she probably didn't say much; she's typically very shy."

"She's the one with the lovely, long, blonde hair, isn't she?" asked Marjorie. "I believe your daughter brought her over to our table on one of her visits."

"Maybe," replied Essie. "Anyway, she dropped by at my request and examined the card. She tells me she believes that my secret admirer is actually the one who made the card."

"What does that mean?" asked Opal sternly. "This card looks like it was purchased. And what about the logo of the card company on the back?"

"Mindy says any good graphic designer could devise a logo like that," replied Essie. She explained the significance of the lack of a bar code on the card. The women were impressed.

"My goodness, Essie," said Marjorie. "This sheds a whole new light on this valentine mystery. If your secret admirer made this beautiful card himself in addition to sending it, he must really be smitten with you!"

"Humph," snorted Essie.

"And he must be a graphic designer," added Opal.

"That's the more important piece of information," agreed Marjorie. "You really need to find out who this man is, Essie."

"I know," replied Essie. "It's driving me crazy to keep looking at it and not be able to figure out who sent it. I keep thinking I must know this man from somewhere and he's just teasing me, trying to get me to figure out who he is—to remember him from somewhere."

"What about his return address on the envelope?" asked Marjorie. "Is there any way you can locate him from that?"

"I don't know," said Essie. "There's just an address, no name. Obviously he wants to maintain his secret identity on the envelope as well as the card."

"Surely there's a way to find out who he is from his address," repeated Opal as she held up the envelope and peered at it. As Marjorie and Essie followed Opal's eyes to the tiny, scratchy handwritten lines on the envelope, Fay, who had been apparently sleeping in her wheelchair on the far side of the table, reached across and grabbed the envelope from Opal's hands.

"Fay!" cried Opal, "I was studying that! Maybe I can figure out the sender from the address."

Fay peered at the address on the envelope. Then, placing it in her lap, she set her coffee cup on its saucer, turned the switch on her chair, and rolled around and down the center aisle of the dining hall.

"Where's she going?" exclaimed Marjorie.

"How should I know?" replied Opal as the three women stared at Fay's retreating form in the distance, now nearing the entrance to the hall.

"Well, wherever she's headed," declared Essie, "I'm following her! She's got my envelope!" Essie shoved her valentine into her walker basket under the seat, rose as quickly as she was able, and rolled her vehicle purposefully out of the dining hall. Opal and Marjorie, not to be left out, grabbed their walkers and joined in the chase. The foursome appeared to be an elderly railroad train with Fay the engine leading a line of cars behind her.

Fay zoomed into the lobby, through the family room, and headed towards the far end of the family room where Happy Haven kept their one computer. This computer was provided for residents' use, but few Happy Haveners were computer literate or even interested in computing, so the little machine stood vacant most of the time. Fay was one of the few residents who knew anything about computers, as Essie and her friends had discovered from previous exploits. They knew that Fay had worked as a research librarian and could track down all sorts of information on the Internet. Essie didn't really understand the Internet, but Fay had assisted her before in her efforts. Essie often wished that she could ask Fay about the Internet and how she knew what she did, but Fay was silent about herself so Essie had learned to accept Fay the way she was.

The women followed Fay and when she arrived at the computer, they gathered around her expecting her to perform some of her computing magic as she had in the past. Fay tucked herself in front of the computer. Essie grabbed the computer chair and sat down beside her. Marjorie pulled over a nearby chair and sat to Fay's right. Opal took a position directly behind Fay. All four women had a good view of the computer screen as Fay booted up and logged onto the Internet.

"What's she doing?" asked Marjorie.

"I believe she's going on the Internet," replied Opal, probably the second most computer savvy of the group. Opal appeared to be able to follow Fay's doings, but she certainly would never be able to conduct such a search herself.

Fay picked up the envelope. She quickly clicked a word at the top of the screen that said "maps." Essie watched as the screen filled with a large map of the United States. Glancing from the envelope to the screen, Fay typed in what appeared to be the return address on the envelope. The women observed what she wrote.

"715 Tingleberry Lane, Boston, Massachusetts, 02106," said Essie. "Is that what it looks like to you, Fay?"

Fay nodded and then glanced from one woman to another. She hit one of the keys on the keyboard and the screen filled with a message that read "no such address listed." Fay frowned and stared harder at the handwritten address.

"I don't think it's Tingleberry," said Marjorie, grabbing the envelope from Fay's hands. "I think that's a 'j' not a 't'!"

"No, it's an 'l' I think," offered Opal, pulling the envelope from Marjorie's hands and squinting at the lettering.

Fay typed furiously and soon she had changed the address on the screen to read 'Jingleberry" and entered that with a punch of a key. The screen provided the same message. There was no Jingleberry Lane in Boston either. Fay repeated the routine using an 'l' instead of a 'j' for the first letter and the results were the same. The three women tried to help Fay by offering different spellings of different words in the return address. Fay diligently checked each and every possible spelling of each and every permutation. After numerous tries, it soon became evident that the return address on the valentine simply did not exist.

"What does this mean?" asked Essie.

Fay sighed, and turning to her friends, gave a shrug.

"I think Fay is saying that this return address doesn't exist. It's fictional," said Opal.

"But why?" asked Essie. "Why would my secret admirer put a non-existent return address on the envelope?"

"Because he doesn't want you to know who he is, obviously," replied Marjorie. "I don't know if that's more romantic or less romantic. Why would your admirer not want you to ever figure out who he is? If he really likes you, you'd think he'd want you to know—ultimately."

"Yes," agreed Essie.

"Maybe there's another reason," suggested Opal. The three seated women turned around and looked up at their tall, serene friend. "Maybe he intentionally put a fake address on the card so that no one would know who he is. Not just Essie."

"That's ridiculous, Opal," declared Marjorie. "Essie is the recipient. Who else would her secret admirer be trying to hide his identity from?"

"I don't know," mused Opal. "The Post Office?"

"What?" said Essie, scowling. "Why would anyone want to keep their identity secret from the Post Office. The Post Office doesn't care who sends me a valentine."

"I can't answer that, Essie," said Opal with a sigh. "However, if you think about it, you're not the only person who won't be able to track your secret admirer now. The purpose of a return address is so that if the Post Office can't deliver a letter, they have a way to return it to the sender. Obviously, if the sender puts a fictitious return address on the envelope, the Post Office will not be able to return the card to the sender."

"I see that, Opal," said Essie. "But, Haley's Comet! What person would NOT want this card back if the Post Office couldn't deliver it to me?"

The women shook their heads and looked forlornly at the computer screen which provided absolutely no information.

"Before we give up totally on this computer thing, Fay," said Essie, "can you try one more thing?"

Fay nodded. Essie picked up the envelope and turned it over.

"Mindy says this card was made for me personally and that the logo on the back is made up. I mean, it's a logo for a company that doesn't really exist. Can we check the company logo, Fay? On the computer?"

Fay took the card from Essie and glanced at the logo on the back. Then she typed the name of the company—Boston Bell Greeting Cards—into a box in the middle of the screen and hit a key. A list of items appeared. Fay ran her finger down each one, shaking her head as she went. Opal followed along. Fay clicked on several of the items, but when the screen filled with text and the women read the various articles, it became clear that none of them were about or even mentioned a "Boston Bell Greeting Card Company."

"Don't worry, Fay," said Essie. "This is not a bad thing. This just shows that there is no Boston Bell Greeting Card Company. It confirms my granddaughter's conjecture that the card was created by one person, not manufactured and then purchased in a store. Now the question is, why? Why did my secret admirer not only send me this card, but why did he go to all the trouble of making it himself in the first place, and creating the impression that it was manufactured by this fictitious company?"

"It's a mystery, Essie," said Opal forlornly. Fay nodded. Marjorie was staring off into space.

"Marjorie," said Essie, giving her typically peppy friend a jab, "where are you?"

"I just remembered," said Marjorie, turning back to the group. "I played cards this morning with Betsy Rollingford."

"That's lovely, Marjorie," noted Opal. "But how does that pertain to Essie's secret admirer valentine?"

"Actually," said Marjorie, "it might pertain a lot. I'm not sure. I happened to mention to the group about your valentine, Essie. Betsy said that she had received a valentine from a secret admirer last year. The way she described it, it sounded a lot like your card."

"Why didn't you tell us this sooner, Marjorie?" asked Essie, annoyed.

"I'm sorry, but it slipped my mind," said Marjorie.

"Slip! Slide! Marjorie!" exclaimed Essie. "Betsy Rollingford? I don't think I know her. What floor is she on?"

"I don't know," said Marjorie, "but I know she plays Bingo. You can probably catch her there tonight!"

"I hope for your sake, I do," snorted Essie as she grabbed her walker and headed out of the family room, leaving her three friends sitting at the computer.

Chapter Seven

"One's first love is always perfect until one meets one's second love."

—Elizabeth Aston

Essie was waiting in the dining hall long before the scheduled start of Bingo that night. She wanted to make certain that she was able to find Betsy Rollingford and have a chat with her about her secret admirer valentine before the Bingo action commenced. Breathing heavily, she tapped her fingers rhythmically on her walker handlebars.

A tall man with grey and black hair entered the room and smiled when he saw Essie sitting alone at one of the tables.

"Essie!" he cried. "You're really early for Bingo!"

"Hello, Dave," she replied politely. Dave was one of the more gregarious men at Happy Haven. That was a polite way to put it. Flirtatious would be another way. Essie might have been flattered with his constant compliments if she hadn't noticed that Dave Esperti tended to pour on the flowery remarks to just about all the female residents.

"My, Essie, you're looking especially stunning tonight," Dave said as he approached.

Essie grimaced. She was not moved by this type of silliness.

"I'm here because I'm trying to track down Betsy Rollingford," she replied, all business.

"Betsy?" asked Dave. "No! And I thought you were waiting for me!" He smiled and laughed flirtatiously as he moved over and took a seat next to her.

"She does play Bingo, doesn't she?"

"Oh, yes," replied Dave, bending in. "She's a regular. You've played Bingo a lot, I thought. You've seen her here."

"Actually, I'm not sure I know who she is," replied Essie uncertainly.

"I'll point her out to you," said Dave, "for a kiss." He wiggled his bushy mustache lasciviously. Essie tried not to gag.

"My kissing days are over, Dave," she said breezily. "I would appreciate it if you'd point her out, though."

As she spoke, residents began to enter the dining hall. Dave moved away from Essie to a more proper distance. He glanced over to the entrance apparently looking for Betsy.

"Hey, Essie," he said while keeping his eyes on the newcomers. "I hear you've got a secret admirer. Is that why I'm getting the brush-off?"

"You're not getting the brush-off, Dave," explained Essie. "No one is getting the brush-off. I treat you as I treat all the men here at Happy Haven. As for the secret admirer, that's what I want to talk to Betsy about. So, please, if you will, continue to be on the lookout."

"Ooops!" he said suddenly. "There she is!" He pointed at a slight woman entering the dining hall. Betsy Rollingford was a small, but regal-looking woman, moving slowly through the use of a three-prong cane. She wore a simple linen dress with a long, bulky white sweater that looked much too big for her tiny frame.

"Thanks, Dave," said Essie. "Here's your kiss." She blew him a discreet kiss from the side of her mouth and headed over towards Betsy Rollingford.

"Betsy," she said. "Are you Betsy Rollingford?"

"Yes," replied the woman cautiously. "That's me."

"Hello," said Essie holding out her hand in greeting. "I'm Essie Cobb. I'm wondering if I might have a word with you before Bingo begins."

"Essie Cobb?" asked the woman. "Oh my! Of course! I know all about you and your adventures! Let's sit over here, shall we?" She motioned to a table near the door and far away from the Bingo set up at the far end of the dining hall. The women sat down at the table. Essie parked her walker nearby.

"Betsy," began Essie, "my friend Marjorie tells me she was playing cards with you today and she mentioned the card I received from a secret admirer."

"Yes, she did!" replied Betsy, smiling. "The way she described your card, Essie, it reminded me of a card I got from a secret admirer last year around Valentine's Day."

"Really?" asked Essie. "What was your card like?"

"Very elaborate, flowery," said Betsy. "It had a little red heart in the center. I'd never seen anything like it since I was a child."

"Was it anything like this?" asked Essie as she opened her walker seat and brought out the card.

"Oh, my!" exclaimed Betsy. "It was just like that! I mean, it was very similar to this. It may have been a different color. I'm not sure. But I do remember all the lace and ribbons and a little puffed up heart just like this one in the center." Essie handed her the card and Betsy examined it carefully.

"And yours was signed 'secret admirer' too?" asked Essie.

"Yes," said Betsy. "I was so excited and curious by the whole thing. It just made my Valentine's Day last year. Probably the best one ever—even better than any with my late husband Donald."

"It is mysterious, isn't it?" said Essie. "Betsy, now that you see my card, do you think there's any possibility that the cards are the same? I mean that maybe they were sent by the same secret admirer?"

"You mean someone we both know here at Happy Haven?" asked Betsy.

"That's a possibility, I guess," agreed Essie. "But my card is postmarked Boston, Massachusetts. Do you remember where your card came from?"

"No, Essie, I'm sorry I don't. I guess I just assumed it came from someone here at Happy Haven."

"Yes, but mine is postmarked Boston. I don't see how anyone here at Happy Haven could send a card from there," said Essie.

"Maybe he could mail it to someone he knows in Boston and the person in Boston mails it from there," suggested the other woman.

"It's possible," agreed Essie. "But why? Why would any man here at Happy Haven go to all the trouble to do that? You're sure you don't remember where your card came from?"

"I really don't remember," said Betsy.

"I don't suppose you kept the card, did you?" asked Essie gingerly.

"I certainly would have. It was so beautiful and so mysterious. I was proud that I had a secret admirer out there even if I couldn't figure out who he was. I definitely planned to keep that card forever."

"But you didn't?" questioned Essie.

"I would have," said Betsy, "but soon after I got it, I put it on the top of my television set. You know, to display it. I really wanted everyone to see it and see that some unknown man somewhere had sent it to me. It was exciting!" She blushed and smiled.

"You displayed it in your apartment," prompted Essie.

"Yes," she said, "I don't remember when it happened, but I remember returning to my room at one point and discovering it missing. I looked everywhere for it. At first, I thought I misplaced it. Then I thought one of the cleaning people took it. But, Essie, that just made no sense. I keep a beautiful diamond and pearl necklace that Donald gave me for our sixtieth wedding anniversary in the top drawer of my dresser. I know the cleaning people have all seen me put it there. They all know it's there. If they wanted to steal something from me, you'd think they'd take that—not a greeting card—no matter how pretty it was."

"So, you never found it?"

"No, I really looked for it too. I asked my aides and the cleaning people. I reported it to Lost and Found and Phyllis tried to help me track it down. But we never found it. I guess I just gave up on it finally. Really, when you think about it, it wasn't worth that much money. It was more the thrill of it, the secret admirer part. I knew I'd never know who he was. He'll always remain a mystery to me. Then, when Marjorie mentioned today about you receiving a valentine from a secret admirer, and told us what it looked like, it got me thinking that your secret admirer card sounded a lot like the one I had received."

"Betsy, how soon after you received the card did it go missing?" asked Essie.

"Oh, very soon. The next day or maybe two days at the most."

"Do you remember receiving the card in your mailbox?" asked Essie.

"I must have received it in my mailbox," answered Betsy. "That's the only place I get mail."

"I mean," said Essie, "did you take the card out of your mailbox yourself? Did someone bring it to you?"

"Oh, I'm sure I got it from my mailbox myself," said Betsy. "I always get my own mail. It's one of my favorite things to do. That sounds pitiful, doesn't it? That picking up my mail every day is one of my favorite activities."

"You aren't saying that you wait at the mailboxes for Phyllis to deliver your mail?"

"No," said Betsy, "I'm not that bad. Besides, she delivers it at different times every day. It always depends when the postman comes. But she's very good about getting the mail into our boxes as soon as it arrives. I've noticed that and I appreciate her efforts."

"Yes," said Essie. "Phyllis is very good about prompt mail delivery." She was contemplating Betsy's observation and wondering how or if it fit into the secret admirer valentine puzzle.

"Is there any other information I can give you, Essie?" asked Betsy. "I'd love to be able to help you solve one of your mysteries. "

"You've helped a huge amount already, Betsy!" cried Essie. "I really think that my secret admirer is or was your secret admirer too. That seems to imply that he's someone we both know. Now I have to figure out how that piece of information fits into the puzzle."

"Well, if you need any more information or if I can help you, just let me know," said Betsy with a smile, patting Essie's hand.

A voice called out, "Ready to start our first round of Bingo! Do you all have your cards?" Essie looked up to see that Sue Barber was standing at the far end of the room with her Bingo paraphernalia ready to call. Essie and Betsy gathered their belongings and headed to the Bingo tables, grabbing several Bingo cards on the way.

Chapter Eight

"Before I met my husband, I'd never fallen in love, though I'd stepped in it a few times."

—Rita Rudner

Essie won fifty cents at Bingo. But other than that financial windfall and her brief discussion with Betsy Rollingford about her stolen valentine, she acquired no additional information that would lead her to identifying her secret admirer.

"Oh, you mysterious little piece of fluff!" she said to the valentine resting in her lap as she sat in her recliner. She idly ran her fingertips over the delicate doily. She could feel the soft, silk ribbon intertwining throughout the little nooks and crannies of the thin lace. Whoever had done this weaving had gone to so much trouble. It was as if the artist had woven or crocheted the ribbon into the doily with the skill of an expert knitter. The filigrees were so thin and the ribbon was so fine, it was truly an art simply to line the edges of the card in this fashion. And yet, despite the delicacy of the work, the card was sturdy. It was well constructed and didn't appear that it would come apart easily.

Essie examined the items on the front of the card more carefully. Her curiosity was in full force. She kept thinking about Betsy and her valentine. If Betsy had received a similar valentine from a secret admirer, and if that valentine

was made by the same person, then that implied that she
and Betsy had the same secret admirer. Now, what were
the odds that some man in Boston would be smitten with
two little old ladies in an assisted living facility hundreds of
miles away? Who could he possibly be? She thought about
Betsy and what she had in common with the woman. Was
there some obvious reason that this unknown admirer
would be infatuated with both of them? What was it about
the two women that might have engaged this unknown
man? Essie thought and thought. The only conclusion she
came to was that she and Betsy both lived at Happy Haven.
That wasn't much of a common bond. Did some man living
on the east coast have a thing for old ladies in facilities in
the middle of the country? And if so, how did he find them?
Why had he selected her and Betsy? None of it made any
sense.

She continued touching the card, running her index finger
over the little pink heart in the center. She lifted it to her
nose and sniffed. She wondered if the heart was a sachet as
Sue Barber had suggested. It didn't appear to have any
odor, so as far as she could tell, that wasn't its purpose.
Even so, she peered at how it was attached. If it was
intended as a sachet, surely the maker expected the
recipient to be able to remove it from the card. Essie tried
to lift up the edges of the heart from the center of the doily.

She drifted off into thought again. *What,* she thought, *of
Fay's attempts to locate the return address and the
company?* Obviously, these unsuccessful efforts pointed
strongly in the direction of her admirer intending to
maintain his anonymity. But why? Why send such a card
and sign it 'secret admirer'? Was he really so shy that he

wanted to convey his affection without revealing his name? And if he was the same person who'd sent Betsy's valentine, just how many women did he secretly admire? Maybe he had dozens, hundreds even, of women in facilities all over the country whom he tantalized with these valentines without ever revealing his actual identity?

Oh my, thought Essie suddenly, *maybe it's one of those senior scams I've heard so much about.* Where unsuspecting senior citizens are coerced into buying some ridiculous product or real estate scheme by devious crooks. But Betsy hadn't mentioned any such occurrence happening to her last year, although Essie hadn't asked her. Essie thought that if Betsy had been approached by someone who connected himself to her secret admirer or claimed to be her secret admirer in order to fleece her, Betsy surely would have made that connection and would have mentioned the fact to Essie. No, if this secret admirer card was the beginning of some sort of ruse to get her money, it was certainly one of the most convoluted approaches that Essie could possibly imagine. She put that thought on a very back burner.

She was still fingering the little heart. As she gently tugged at the edges, she noticed the glue around the base starting to give way. *Oh, dear,* she thought, *I don't want to break it. If I pull too hard, the filling might leak out.* However, it was too late and with her last pull, the small silk heart detached from its base and popped into Essie's hand. She carefully lifted it up and turned it over. The back of the heart was sewn with the smallest hand stitches she had ever seen. On top of the stitches, a layer of glue provided additional protection. Indeed, the bottom of the heart was rock solid.

It was possible to remove the heart from its base, but it would be virtually impossible to open the heart from behind. *It probably was intended as a sachet*, Essie reasoned, *even if it didn't smell good to her.* It was sturdy enough to remain indefinitely in someone's drawer without accidentally breaking and spilling its contents out on one's clothes.

Essie touched the center of the card where the heart had been and she felt a sticky substance. It appeared that the heart had been fastened with a type of glue that would allow it to be reattached, so Essie carefully placed the little heart in the center of the card and gently pressed it down. The heart appeared to stay put when Essie held the card up to test to see if the heart would fall off. It didn't.

Her nighttime aide, Lorena, stuck her head in the door.

"Miss Essie," she greeted Essie warmly. "You want to get ready for bed, or are you plannin' some late night rendezvous with that secret admirer of yours?" Lorena came in and closed the door.

"Oh, Lorena," said Essie, "don't tell me you heard about the valentine too?"

"Miss Essie, honey," said Lorena, busily getting Essie's nighttime pills from her kitchen cupboard, "there ain't nobody at HH who don't know about your admirer!"

"Oh, no!" cried Essie. "Can't a girl have a boyfriend without it being broadcast to the world?"

"Not here, she can't!" said Lorena knowingly as she brought Essie's pills to her, along with a glass of water. Essie took the pills and water and swallowed them without a fuss. Lorena smiled broadly. "Good for you, girl! You usually moan and groan about those big ones!"

"I have other more pressing issues on my mind tonight, Lorena," noted Essie, as she handed the glass back to her aide.

"You mean you trying to find that mystery boyfriend of yours?"

"You haven't seen one hanging around outside have you?" asked Essie. She and Lorena always liked to tease each other about their love lives or lack thereof. Lorena had been married for years and she and her husband had five children. She had always made it clear that her idea of romance was when her husband just left her alone.

"It seems Betsy Rollingford got a secret admirer valentine last year," said Essie. "It was a lot like mine but she misplaced it." Essie was loathe to say it was stolen, because she assumed that Lorena would infer that she meant one of the staff stole it.

"That's not good," said Lorena, still standing beside Essie's recliner. "That the card?" she asked, looking down at the valentine in Essie's lap.

"The very one," said Essie.

"Hmmm," said Lorena, peering at it from her standing position. "That about the fanciest card I ever seen!"

"Me too!" agreed Essie, picking up the card and handing it over to Lorena.

"My goodness, Miss Essie," she said as she opened the card and read the inside. "This man, he flat out mad about you!"

"I'm not so sure, Lorena," said Essie, shaking her head. "If he really cared about me, why be so mysterious? Wouldn't he want me to know who he is?"

"He shy," said Lorena as if that answered all of Essie's questions and put the entire mystery to bed. She handed the card back to Essie. "Shy men, they do weird things. They a lot of shy men at HH." She headed into the bedroom.

"Oh, Lorena!" said Essie, laughing and calling out to her. "I don't know about that!"

"I do, Miss Essie!" replied her aide, as she returned from the bedroom with Essie's pajamas. "Lordy, do I wish I had me a shy man. My Bernie! He not shy. Not shy at all. Nope. We got five kids, Miss Essie. A little more shy not bother me at all." Lorena rolled her eyes as she helped Essie out of her trousers and into her nighttime attire.

"Lorena," said Essie, "I do appreciate your insight, but I don't think my secret admirer is shy. I think there's a totally different reason for his secrecy."

"No, he just shy!" maintained Lorena. She finished helping Essie get ready for bed and then headed out to her next resident. "Mark my words, Miss Essie. This one shy man who love you!" She shook her finger at Essie as the door closed behind her. Lorena's words of wisdom did little to calm Essie's concerns. Now, in addition to her aide's personality assessment of her secret admirer, Essie was concerned that Lorena had seen the card. It appeared that most, if not all of Happy Haven, now knew she had received a card from a secret admirer. Probably a good portion had figured out or could figure out that she probably kept it in her walker basket. She did keep many of her important possessions in her walker seat—as did many Happy Haven residents who used walkers. It wasn't that Essie feared that Lorena would steal her card. But she did worry that her gregarious aide might accidentally mention the card to one person too many. Essie did not want to lose her card as Betsy Rollingford had.

She rolled into her bedroom, still contemplating these issues, her valentine housed safely in her walker basket. She pulled down her covers and slid under her sheets, pulling her walker close by. This was where she usually kept her trusty vehicle, because she often needed it in the middle of the night for quick bathroom visits. Now, however, there was a second reason to keep her walker close to her bed. If someone did try to slip into her apartment in the middle of the night and steal the card, Essie wanted to be prepared. She wasn't exactly certain what she'd do if someone actually did enter her bedroom and try to take something out of her walker basket. Really, all she wanted was to know who it was. She figured that if someone took it, it would be someone who either was the secret admirer or who knew who the secret admirer was. In a way, Essie was actually hoping someone would come and take the card. Then this mystery would be solved. Maybe. It didn't really dawn on her that someone breaking into her apartment and stealing something from her was actually dangerous and if she attempted to intervene, even by trying to discover the person's identity, she could endanger her own welfare.

She lay down and tried to sleep. Eventually she drifted off. When she awoke in the middle of the night with an urgent need to visit her toilet, she first opened her walker seat. The valentine was still there in its cream-colored envelope. She even peeked inside to be sure someone hadn't come in and removed the card from the envelope, but the original card was definitely there. No one had come to get it. She made her quick bathroom trip and returned to bed. This process was repeated several more times throughout the night, and each time when she awakened and checked in her basket the card was still there.

Chapter Nine

"Passion makes the world go round. Love just makes it a safer place."

—Ice T

At breakfast the next morning, Essie was anxious to tell her tablemates what she had learned from Betsy Rollingford. Her valentine remained snug in the basket of her walker seat beside her.

The women were uncharacteristically quiet as they savored Happy Haven cinnamon rolls that the chef made fresh once a week. Essie had slathered hers with more butter than she typically used, but she figured she deserved this little addition to one of her favorite treats. After all, she'd been hard at work trying to figure out a puzzling mystery.

"Butter on your cinnamon roll," observed Opal. "Essie, isn't that overkill? I mean there must be a pound of butter in these rolls to begin with." Opal was nibbling her roll delicately, patting her lips every so often with her napkin. Essie felt a drool of butter run down the side of her chin.

"It's a special treat," replied Essie, slurping up the dribble of butter. "I've been working hard trying to figure out this valentine thing."

"Oh!" cried Marjorie, "did you find out who he is, Essie?" Her romantic friend was now thoroughly engaged in the conversation. Anything that involved men, romance, or gossip would always get Marjorie's juices flowing. "What about Betsy? Did you ever find her?"

"I did," replied Essie, setting down her roll and wiping her fingers with her napkin. "She got a valentine last year, much like mine, she says."

"You showed her yours?" asked Opal with similar curiosity.

"Yes, Opal," replied Essie, still slightly annoyed with what she considered Opal's bossiness. "I show you mine, you show me yours."

"Did you see hers?" asked Marjorie with enthusiasm.

"No," said Essie. "She didn't have it."

"You mean she didn't have it with her?" asked Opal.

"No," said Essie. "I mean she didn't have it anymore. "

"She didn't throw it away, did she?" cried Marjorie. "I would never get rid of such a beautiful expression of love, especially from an unknown admirer."

"No, Marjorie," continued Essie, "she didn't throw it away. It was stolen. She put it on her television set shortly after she received it and not long after that it went missing."

"Oh, she probably just misplaced it," suggested Opal. "I can't imagine anyone wanting to steal some greeting card from a resident."

"Maybe a resident took it!" exclaimed Marjorie. "Maybe one of her friends who was jealous!"

"Marjorie," said Essie, "it was displayed in her room. You're suggesting another resident went into her apartment and took this card from the top of her television set?"

"It's possible," replied Marjorie sheepishly.

"It's more likely that a staff member took it," suggested Opal.

"That's what I'm thinking," agreed Essie. "We all keep our rooms unlocked. Aides and cleaning people come and go into our rooms, sometimes when we're there and sometimes when we're not. I'm sure it would be easy for a staff member to just slip into Betsy's room and grab that card without anyone noticing it at all."

"But why, Essie?" asked Marjorie. "Why would a staff member do that?"

"That's what I can't figure out," replied Essie. "Betsy said she had some valuable items in her room." Essie didn't mention exactly what Betsy had mentioned or where it was located. She figured she owed the woman this much discretion. "She couldn't understand why someone would take a paper greeting card but not anything valuable."

"You'd better keep an eye on your card, Essie," admonished Opal, glancing over at Essie's walker.

"Don't worry," said Essie. "It will never leave my side. If anyone tries to take it, they'll have to come through me first."

"Oh, Essie!" cried Marjorie. "That sounds dangerous! I hope you don't do anything foolish just to protect a valentine!"

"Are you even sure that there's a connection between your card and Betsy's? They could be from different people," said Opal.

"No," said Essie. "I showed my card to Betsy and she remembered her card very well. She said they were practically the same. Maybe different colors, but she remembered the same doily, ribbons, and little heart in the center. I really think she received a card just like mine."

"That means that the same person sent it," said Marjorie, her eyes wide with realization.

"Yes," agreed Essie. "Her secret admirer is my secret admirer."

"So what does that mean, Essie?" questioned Opal, frowning. "Is this man in love with lots of women here at Happy Haven? He lives in Boston, right?"

"Right, Opal," replied Essie. "I don't know what it means. But I do think that there's more going on here than meets the eye. I don't know who this secret admirer is, but I intend to find out. Betsy never received any other card or call from a secret admirer. She is still mystified by it. And I'm sure her admirer is the same as mine. And since her card was stolen, I can only guess that someone may attempt to steal my card too. So, my intention is to guard it so that if anyone tries to take it, I will learn who they are and find out why they are doing this."

"That sounds potentially dangerous, Essie," said Opal. "I agree with Marjorie."

"Oh, stop it, you two!" said Essie, hands up. "I'm not going to do anything valiant. If anyone tries to take the card, I'll just let them. But I'll observe who they are so I can track them down later."

"So you say, Essie," noted Marjorie, shaking her head. "You be careful! I don't want to lose one of my best friends!" A tear welled up in Marjorie's eye and she patted it with her napkin. Then, she shoved the rest of her cinnamon roll in her mouth in an obvious attempt to deflect attention from her outburst.

The women became silent as they sipped their coffee and enjoyed the last few bites of their cinnamon rolls. Eventually, they departed the dining hall and Essie made her mid-morning stop at the mailboxes. Apparently, the mailman had arrived early this morning, and Phyllis had already delivered the mail to the boxes. Essie reached in and pulled out a handful of flyers and ads. There were no valentines in her mailbox this morning and she wondered how long the mail had been in the boxes. She glanced over to the front desk and noticed that Phyllis was there busily working with a sign-up list on the counter.

Essie shoved her mail into her walker seat basket and pushed herself over to the front desk.

"Good morning, Miss Essie," said Phyllis, looking up from her duty. She appeared to be counting the number of residents who had signed up for some activity. Essie moved closer to Phyllis.

"Hello, Phyllis," she said, her head bent close to the desk clerk. "I see you already have the mail out. The mailman must have come early today."

"He did," replied Phyllis. "Some days he's early. Some days late. But whenever he arrives, Essie, I always drop what I've been doing here and distribute the mail to the boxes. I know how important it is to our residents to get their mail each day."

"There isn't any pattern to when the mailman arrives, then?" asked Essie.

"Not that I'm aware of," replied Phyllis, biting her lip. "I've never thought about it. Maybe there is. I just don't know what the pattern would be, Essie. Possibly he's later on Mondays because the mail piles up over a weekend. I don't know. I never really stopped to analyze it. Is there a reason you need to know?"

"Oh, no!" said Essie, laughing. "You know me, Phyllis! I'm just curious. I noticed how early he was yesterday—so much earlier than today. I was just wondering."

"I can't really say why," said Phyllis. "Let me see, it's ten thirty and I just finished putting the mail in the boxes. Yesterday, I believe I had it all up by...hmm...maybe nine thirty. You're right. It was earlier yesterday. I don't have any idea why."

"So, what you're saying is that the mailman arrives at different times every day, but that you put the mail up as soon as he delivers it, no matter when."

"Absolutely!" said Phyllis. "I would never just let the mail sit on the counter undelivered. I always distribute it as soon as it gets here. Of course, he always gets here in the morning. I've never known the mailman to arrive any later than noon. And usually no later than, let's say, eleven."

"Hmm," said Essie, pondering this information. "No later than eleven. And how early might he arrive?"

"That's a good question," replied Phyllis. "Of course, he couldn't get in the building before six because it's locked. But I don't believe he's ever been here that early! Probably the earliest he's ever been here was...maybe nine or eight thirty."

"So, the window for the mailman's arrival is somewhere between nine and eleven," said Essie almost to herself. "A two hour window."

"Yes," said Phyllis, "that sounds about right. Why do you ask?"

"It's that old curiosity of mine again," laughed Essie. "You know us old ladies; we don't have much else to do with ourselves than calculate the arrival time of the local postman." She gave Phyllis a forced laugh. Phyllis joined in for a moment. As she was about ready to depart, Essie turned from the front desk as Santos whizzed by her with a covered food tray heading towards her hallway off the family room again. Essie said farewell to Phyllis and pushed her walker after the waiter and down her hallway.

As she turned into her hallway, she saw Santos at the far end where the hallway dead-ended. He made a quick turn to the left. Essie contemplated whether to continue to her own room which was a few doors down on the left or follow Santos. She quickly decided to follow the waiter. She wished Santos had turned right because the hallway on the right continued only a short distance. There were just a few apartments down that portion of the hallway and Essie knew all the residents in them. Unfortunately, Santos had turned left. Taking this route led him down a segment of hallway that ran the full length of the Happy Haven building. Essie thought she knew a good number of the residents who lived down this hallway but she wasn't exactly certain which room went with which resident.

She rolled her walker quickly down the corridor to the end where Santos had disappeared from sight. Cautiously, she peeked around the corner and glanced surreptitiously down the left-hand side. She saw Santos's back walking in the distance. As she followed him with her eyes, he suddenly stopped and knocked on a door on the left. The door opened immediately and Santos slipped inside.

Now whose apartment is that? thought Essie. Did she dare roll down the hall and read the resident's name on the door? *No,* she thought. *Santos will probably just drop off the tray and then come back out.* She waited and waited. Several minutes went by and Santos did not come out of the room. *Now, why is he staying so long after delivering a food tray?* she asked herself. She counted the number of doors down the hallway where Santos had entered. Keeping the location of the apartment firmly in her mind, she turned around and pushed her walker back towards her own room and past it and out to the family room where she snatched a comfy, inconspicuous chair. She sat down and waited, her eyes on the hallway, waiting for Santos to return.

Chapter Ten

"Nothing takes the taste out of peanut butter quite like unrequited love."

—Charles M. Schulz

As she sat in the family room, totally focused on catching Santos when he returned from delivering the food tray, she failed to notice a group of card players at a table nearby. As her eyes continued to squint towards the end of the corridor watching for the waiter, she began to recognize the voices of several residents she knew. She saw several residents and staff members enter and exit the hallway, but no Santos.

"Essie Cobb!" called out a familiar voice. "You can't hide over there in that big chair!"

Essie glanced over and immediately saw Dave Esperti waving at her to join the group of card players. *Curses and epithets!* she thought. *There goes my attempt at spying.* With a sigh, she pulled herself out of the comfortable armchair and rolled over to the group of men and women sitting at a small card table. In addition to Dave, she also recognized Hubert Darby. She didn't know the two female players.

"Get any more fancy valentines from your secret admirer?" asked Dave. Essie frowned. Even though she knew that most of Happy Haven was apparently aware of her unknown beau, she really didn't appreciate Dave Esperti teasing her about it.

"No, I didn't, Dave," replied Essie perfunctorily. She smiled briefly at the group and returned her attention to the hallway. Several people disappeared at the far end around the corner. *Oh, no!* she thought. *I didn't see them. Where did they come from? Maybe I've missed Santos.* She was annoyed that Dave and the card players had distracted her from her task. Now she might have missed Santos returning down the hallway. Was it safe to check who the resident was in the apartment in which he had gone or not? Essie was totally lost in thought.

"Hey, Essie!" yelled Dave. "Cat got your tongue? So smitten with your new fellow that you can't even talk to us regular guys here?" Essie tore herself from her hallway watch and smiled sweetly at Dave and the group.

"Of course not, Dave," she said. "You know, just distracted. A senior moment." She knew that any fault or flaw at Happy Haven could be easily dismissed with the 'senior moment' excuse. She used it herself quite frequently although there was usually some other reason. Essie didn't have many senior moments.

The ladies at the table laughed and Hubert Darby, who was also one of the card players, blushed. Or at least Essie thought she saw him blush.

"Essie," said one of the women. "Ignore Dave. He's a terrible tease. I, for one, think your secret admirer is one of the most romantic things I've heard of in ages. I'm Hazel." She touched Essie's hand warmly. Hubert scowled and stared at his cards more intently.

"I do too," added the other lady card player. "I'm Mildred. It's nice to know that there's at least one man out there who knows how to romance a lady!" She gave pointed looks at both Dave and Hubert. The two men stayed quiet.

"Actually, Essie," said Hazel. "I'm jealous of you! I never even got any kind of romantic valentine from my husband when he was alive."

"Me neither," agreed Mildred. "Do you have any idea who he is?"

"No," said Essie. Dave and Hubert had apparently bowed out of this conversation. "I wish I did, but it's a mystery."

"That makes it even more romantic, don't you think?" asked Mildred quietly. She gestured for Essie to come closer. Essie hesitated. She wanted to be polite, but she also wanted to keep her eyes on the hallway so she could see Santos when he returned.

"Could we see it?" asked Hazel shyly. Essie looked back and forth from one woman to the other. She really didn't want to display her card around Happy Haven like some wild life trophy from a safari. Like she had bagged an unknown man and this card was the result.

"Please, Essie," pleaded Mildred.

"I really..." began Essie.

"A little bird says you carry it everywhere with you," whispered Hazel.

"Hey, Hazel," interjected Dave. "Essie doesn't want to show you the card. Leave her alone!" He slammed a card down on the table. "Trump!" he declared and then slid down in his chair and crossed his arms. The women bristled and Hubert Darby looked up at Essie with a soulful glance.

Essie felt uncomfortable that she now suddenly found herself in the middle of this dispute. The women at the table were obviously excited about Essie's valentine and her secret admirer, the men apparently annoyed, possibly even threatened. How could she dispel the bad vibes that she felt from this group and avoid prompting a mini-battle?

"Oh, Dave!" she declared. "Don't worry! I don't mind showing the card to Mildred and Hazel. I've shown it to just about everyone else here at Happy Haven!" She lifted her walker seat and produced the cream-colored envelope that remained on the top of her precious pile. She handed it to Hazel who pulled out the card inside and examined it. Mildred reached across the table and grabbed it.

"Oh, let me see!" she cried. The two women gushed over the valentine while Dave and Hubert fumed.

"It's not all that amazing," noted Dave. "I've seen better."

"What do you mean you've *seen* better?" asked Hazel. She clutched the card to her chest so Dave couldn't see it.

"I mean I've given my share of fancy cards, Hazel," replied Dave, "and some of them have been a lot nicer than this one!"

"Oh, really?" said Hazel. "I don't think I've ever seen any valentine quite so elaborate as this." She held the card with both hands and brought it close to her face. Essie grimaced in fear that the little heart would fall off with all of the handling it was getting, but the glue in the center of the doily held strong.

"Do you have any idea who your admirer is, Essie?" asked Mildred.

"No," replied Essie. "I wish I did."

"Just forget him, whoever he is," continued Dave, now full of his original confidence. "I told you, Essie, I'm the man for you!" He winked at her. Hubert's eyes widened. He looked over at the flowery card from Essie's secret admirer.

"Hubert," exclaimed Mildred. "What's wrong?" Indeed, Hubert Darby's face was a bright shade of red and his mouth looked as if it might explode with some horrible swear word at any moment.

"Hubert," added Hazel, "are you okay?"

Hubert grabbed his suspenders and looked at Essie. Then he looked at the valentine in Hazel's hands. His hands and shoulders shaking uncontrollably, he ran from the table.

"What's wrong with him?" asked Dave.

Essie was shocked to see that the discussion of her secret admirer valentine had brought out so many emotions in the residents at the table. She had certainly not expected Hubert Darby to react in such a dramatic way. Now she felt terrible. Hubert had always been sweet to her and always a gentleman. The last thing she ever wanted to do was hurt his feelings. Now apparently, she had. She looked up and only then remembered her plan to track Santos's coming down her hallway. With all the excitement over her valentine, she had completely lost track of the people coming and going from the hallway.

"I think Hubert's sweet on you, Essie," whispered Mildred. "I'd like to know just what you do to get so many men to adore you!"

"Nothing!" retorted Essie. "Nothing at all. In fact, if anything, I discourage them. I was a lot happier before this strange person sent me this valentine and I truly wish he'd never sent it in the first place!"

"You're kidding!" said Hazel. "I wouldn't feel that way. I'm jealous of you, Essie."

"See, Essie," noted Dave, now having disposed of his cards, the hand evidently over with Hubert's departure, "the women here all want to be you! And the men all love you! At least, I know I do!" Dave stood elegantly, bowed to Essie in a majestic fashion, and then departed.

Left alone with just the two lady card players, Essie took the seat that Dave had just deserted. Turning her back on the hallway, she faced the females, giving up her attempt to track Santos. *I guess I'll have to check out that room later*, she thought.

She sat with Mildred and Hazel, smiling politely while the two women continued to examine her valentine. Much later, when the women had apparently tired of looking at the card, Essie took her valentine and returned it to her basket. Rising and heading down her hallway, she glanced at her wristwatch. *Oh, my! I spent over an hour sitting there chatting with those four! Surely that's enough time for Santos to have left that room. I obviously missed him.*

As she rolled closer to her own doorway, she made a split second decision and continued on down the hallway. At the end of the corridor, she rounded the corner to the left. The corridor was empty. Essie pushed her walker slowly down the carpeted floor, counting and checking each doorway as she went. Her mind still contained a visual and mental picture of the doorway into which Santos had gone. *It was the fifth one on the left*, she said to herself. When she arrived at the doorway where she was certain that Santos had delivered the tray earlier, she paused her walker and stood at the door so she could read the name plate.

Grace Bloom, she read to herself. *I know Grace. I could swear that she's not ill. She was at supper last night, I think.*

Essie hesitated as she tried to decide whether or not to knock. If she knocked and Grace was home, what excuse would she give for coming to visit? She pondered all sorts of excuses but none came to mind. She knew who Grace was but the two women didn't share in any activities at Happy Haven so it wasn't as if she could come calling on her about anything specific. Did they have anyone in common? Anyone she could reference when she spoke to the woman? *No,* she thought. *I don't know who she knows and I can't even remember how I know who she is.*

What the hedges! she said to herself finally. *Here goes!*

She knocked firmly on the door. There was a brief commotion sound inside and suddenly the door opened a crack and Grace Bloom's head peeked out.

"Yes?" she asked.

"Grace Bloom?" asked Essie.

"That's me!" replied the woman, hanging on the door almost defensively.

"I...I...I'm Essie Cobb," said Essie. "I heard you were ill."

"Ill?" cried Grace, laughing. "Where did you get that idea?" The woman's lively eyes sparkled behind her horn-rimmed glasses.

"I...I... believe I heard one of the kitchen workers mention it," lied Essie.

"They must have been thinking of some other Grace," said Grace Bloom. "Not me!"

"So, you're not sick?" asked Essie tentatively, stretching her head around in an attempt to see beyond the door and into Grace Bloom's apartment. It was impossible. Grace had a tight grip on her door and was not apparently going to open it for anyone.

"No!" replied Grace. She closed her mouth and stared at Essie as if to say, *so what?*

"Well," said Essie suddenly. "That's wonderful!" She turned her walker abruptly and headed back down the hallway.

Rockwell 89

Chapter Eleven

"To fear love is to fear life, and those who fear life are already three parts dead."

—Bertrand Russell

That was a dead-end in more ways than one, thought Essie as she rolled her walker into her apartment. She couldn't get the picture of Grace Bloom out of her mind. The woman had clutched her front door as if it were a lifeboat. Obviously she wasn't sick, but what was going on? And why did Santos bring her a breakfast tray when Grace obviously wasn't ill or incapacitated. Essie moved over to her rocker/recliner and slid down into the cushion. She stared ahead, through the blinds on her outside window that fronted onto a small patio in the center of Happy Haven. She could see a squirrel zip up one of the snow-covered elm trees. She pushed her chair back and forth as if in rhythm with her fluctuating thoughts.

Her eyes drifted to the top of her television set in the corner by the window. Essie didn't keep many items on top of her TV because she worried that they might get too hot and catch fire. She did have a set of porcelain birds—each one a different type—arranged in a casual pattern. The cardinal and the bluebird usually were on the left and the robin and blue jay were on the right. *What?* She looked again. Somehow, the little decorative birds had apparently changed positions. Now, the cardinal and the robin were on the left and the bluebird and the blue jay were on the right. She knew that wasn't how she had arranged them. Or had she? She was ninety years old. She supposed it was possible that she had put her bird collection in a different order and forgotten about it, but she truly didn't think so. Ceramic birds didn't walk about on the top of a television set all by themselves. They needed help.

Essie let her eyes roam around her small apartment. From where she sat in her recliner against the far wall between her desk and the end table by her two-seater sofa, she could see every part of her little living room. She could also see her small kitchenette if she turned her head far to the right and looked over her shoulder. In this position she could also see the hallway that led to her bathroom and bedroom.

Was anything else different or just the birds? She started with the television set and moved around her living room. Next to the right of the TV was her antique desk—not the one she used every day, but a fancy one she had brought with her from her personal furniture and that she used primarily to store important papers and items. The little desk with the curlicued legs had a front that closed and locked with a key that Essie kept with her at all times in her purse in her walker basket. On top of the desk stood a glass-covered golden clock that one of her grandsons had given her. It appeared to be slightly off-center. Essie was always very careful to place it in the direct center of the top of her antique desk. Next to this desk was another armchair. This one was gold and it circled around on rollers. Marjorie always liked to sit there when she visited. Several stuffed animals that Essie had received as prizes from various games and contests at Happy Haven resided on this chair—always ready to greet incoming visitors with their cheery faces. Essie typically had the purple bear sitting on the left and the brown bear sitting on the right of the seat cushion. Now they were reversed. *Hmmm*, she said to herself, pondering the change in her stuffies' positions.

She continued her examination of her living room, looking around carefully from one furniture item to the next. Immediately to Essie's left was her regular desk. On this large piece of furniture, Essie kept all other important papers and reminders. She had a calendar propped upright in the back center of the desk. The calendar was open to the month of February, and Essie had penciled in various appointments she had scheduled during the month. She also had a container of pens and pencils on the top right hand corner and a stack of papers in the lower right hand corner. At least, that's where those items were supposed to be. As she peered over her shoulder, she could tell that all of her desk items were just slightly out of place. The pile of papers on the right which included many envelopes and cards that she had received and wanted to keep was dramatically changed from the way it was as she last remembered it. The cards and envelopes in the pile had been rearranged and sort of shoved back together in a haphazard fashion.

There didn't appear to be anything different about her recliner or the sofa. Maybe some of the throw pillows were arranged differently on the short couch, but Essie couldn't tell for sure. She was always puffing the pillows and placing them strategically on the sofa for maximum effect. She had read once that pillows placed at an angle in the corner of a sofa would make it appear larger—and as her sofa was about as small as sofas came, she was willing to do almost anything to increase its apparent size. *No*, she thought, *the sofa looks the same.*

Next to the far side of the sofa was a large container which was originally intended for coal by a fireplace, but which Essie used to store magazines. As far as she could see, the magazines appeared to be the same as were in the container before. *The one on top might be different*, she mused. She wasn't certain. Next to the magazine container was another chair, this one blue. There was a lace crocheted doily on the back of the chair. It was folded up—not the way Essie would ever have left it.

The window to the outside was directly behind the blue chair. Essie now realized that the blinds were slightly closed, not open to bring in the sunshine as she typically left them. Had someone come in and changed her blinds? Of course, she realized, cleaning people often entered her apartment and cleaned. But they generally didn't change the location or arrangement of any of a resident's belongings. In fact, she couldn't remember any time in the past where a staff member cleaning ever did anything to affect anything in any of her rooms at all. This was very strange.

Essie pushed herself out of her recliner and rolled herself into her bedroom. Her bed looked pretty much the same as it had that morning. Yes, the bed was made. DeeDee, her morning aide, usually did that for her. The coverlet looked very much like it did every day after DeeDee made it. Moving over to her end table, Essie sat on her bed so she could see the items on her nightstand better. Here she kept a lot of personal items—her phone, a small phone book, a glowing light, some cough drops, and other things she felt she might need in the middle of the night. She could clearly remember how she had left these personal items this morning. All of the items appeared to have been rearranged. Oh, they still had the appearance of casual disarray, but they were not the same as they had been this morning. Essie rolled over to the end table on the other side of her bed. Here she kept some books and other personal papers. These items too were changed or had been moved. She was certain.

She looked around her bedroom attempting to see any other obvious changes. The top of her long, low dresser caught her attention and she rolled over. There were framed photographs, two decorative lamps, and some other small china items. Essie's keen eye alerted her to small differences in the arrangement of all of them.

She rolled into her tiny bathroom. Expecting to see her bathroom in upheaval, she saw only the same small changes here that she had seen in her living room and in her bedroom. The items on her sink had been rearranged. Her toothbrush and tube of toothpaste were still on the left of the sink, but they were sitting at different angles than she had placed them this morning. She opened the cabinet doors under her sink. Her containers of adult diapers which she hated to use, but did rely on from time to time, were still there but had been turned sideways. Her package of toilet paper had also changed position.

Essie had seen enough. She pushed her walker slowly back into her living room and lowered herself into her recliner. Shaking her head, she thought, *someone has been going through my things.* Her mind contemplated this invasion of her privacy. It was definitely more than just a cleaning crew doing their regular job. This was someone who had come into her apartment while she was away and rummaged through her private belongings. It didn't take a genius to figure out that the person must have been looking for the secret admirer valentine. *The same thing probably happened to Betsy Rollingford last year. Only, with Betsy, the person found the card without much searching. In my case, the person had no idea where it was so they went through everything, hoping to find it. And, of course, they didn't find it because I've had that valentine with me ever since I received it. Of course, the thief doesn't know that.*

Doggone dog biscuits! Why should one little card cause so much trouble? She reached over to her walker and lifted up the seat. She grabbed the valentine and removed it from its envelope. *I'm so annoyed with you, Mr. Secret Admirer! Why couldn't you just sign your real name? What's all this secrecy about anyway? And why me? What did I ever do to you?*

She rocked back and forth furiously in a steady rhythm, rubbing the card with annoyance. Suddenly, she stopped and pulled up on the little heart in the center. Sure enough, the original glue was still holding. She pulled harder. Eventually, the heart popped up and away from the card and into Essie's hands. She turned the heart over and reexamined the back—the thick layer of glue and the fine line of stitches down the middle of it. She reached over to her desk and opened the top right hand drawer and brought out a nail file. Using the tip of the file, she began to saw and poke at the back of the heart. Slowly, after extensive effort, a small opening was created. Essie used the tip of the file to poke inside the little heart. She could feel the interior.

I wonder what's inside? she mused. She poked deeper. Sue Barber had suggested that the heart might be filled with sawdust or sachet powder. She couldn't tell. Maybe it was sand. She brought the heart up close to her nose to see if she could smell anything now that a small opening had been created and the material inside had access to the outside air. No odor emanated from the heart. *Why had the card's creator made it so difficult to open the little heart?* Essie's imagination went wild. *Maybe it wasn't just sawdust or even a sachet. Maybe the heart contains jewels! Maybe a cache of diamonds!*

Essie sawed furiously with her nail file, attempting to widen the small opening at the back of the heart so she could see what was inside. Eventually, with her diligent efforts, some of the small stitches gave way along with the glue, and a tiny opening appeared, revealing the contents. As Essie peered inside wondering what she'd see, a puff of fine white powder blew upwards and slowly drifted onto her lap.

Chapter Twelve

"O, then, what graces in my love do dwell, that he hath turn'd a
heaven unto hell!"

—Shakespeare

"Wiggling weasels!" she exclaimed.

Essie froze as she stared at the thin layer of powder on the
knees of her trousers. She didn't move. She couldn't move.
What in the world was it? It certainly didn't appear to be
normal stuffing material. She recalled how once one of her
stuffed bears that kept watch over her living room from the
armchair across from her recliner had developed a hole on
his bottom. His stuffing had started to ooze out and she
had to get out her needle and thread and sew up his
wound. Her bear's insides were nothing like this. He
seemed to be full of bits of foam rubber, as she recalled. Of
course, this little heart was a different situation and she
reasoned that there were many possible materials that
people could use to stuff things. But as she stared at the
powder now forming little rivulets in the creases of her
pants, she couldn't imagine what the substance might be
and why her secret admirer would use it to fill the tiny
heart.

Without moving, she attempted to peer into the heart. She
wished she could reach over to her desk and get her
flashlight out of her desk drawer but she didn't want to
move and disturb the powder on her lap. Although she
couldn't see inside, it appeared to be full of the substance.

She held the heart gingerly, not wishing to disperse any more of the material than she already had.

This powder was simply not what she'd expected to find inside of the heart. She'd anticipated sawdust or sand. She stared at the powder on her lap and the few grains she could see within the heart. It certainly wasn't flour. It might be sand but she thought it was much too white and too fine for that.

Suddenly her mind brought up images of news reports from years before. She remembered those horrible days when some maniac had mailed anthrax powder to various government officials and the entire country had come to a virtual standstill as law enforcement attempted to track down a mass murderer who remained elusive. Could this be like that? Could this fine white powder in her little heart be some deadly poison sent to her by a terrorist? Her entire body froze as the possibility engulfed her. She considered the possibilities. It had been sent in the mail. The sender was unknown. She and her friends had already attempted to track down her 'secret admirer' with no results. If this was an attempt at terrorism, surely the terrorist had covered his tracks.

Essie, you elephant! she scolded herself. *Why in the world would some international terrorist target you? You're just a little old lady in an assisted living facility. You're not an important political or government official or military leader. You are probably the least likely of targets of a terrorist. And besides,* she reasoned, *if this was terrorism, the terrorist surely was making it hard for you to even be affected by the poison. I mean, he has it so thoroughly wrapped up in this heart that it would be unlikely that anyone would ever tumble to the fact that this substance was inside unless they were actively looking for it. It's probably nothing. It's probably just some simple household ingredient that this person had on hand.*

Okay, then what is it? Why can't I come up with any probable answer? What should I do?

Essie sat rigid in her recliner, not moving any part of her body as she focused intently on the powder on her lap. She thought if she concentrated hard enough, the answer would come to her and she would be able to put an end to the frightening possibility that the white powder was dangerous. As she pondered, she realized that if the powder truly was poisonous, she was making matters worse by continuing to sit there as the fine white grains were no doubt drifting into the atmosphere and ultimately into her lungs. She attempted to breathe more shallowly.

This is ridiculous! I have to do something about this. I can't continue to sit here immobile with this stuff all over me. Should I call Phyllis at the front desk? she wondered. *No. What could she do? If this truly is poison, then I will have just exposed an additional person to danger.* She also realized that she couldn't just stand up and brush herself off and then go somewhere looking for help. If she did and if the powder was poison, she would be leaving a trail of death throughout Happy Haven. No, she would have to remain exactly where she was and have help come to her. At least, until she knew for certain that the material on her lap was not dangerous. *Better to be safe than sorry,* her own mother's words echoed in her mind.

Ultimately, Essie realized what she would have to do. No one at Happy Haven could or should be exposed to this problem. It was her dilemma and she would have to solve it. Cautiously, she reached out for her telephone on the end table to her left. Her movement sent particles of powder aloft and swirling around her knees. She turned her head, attempting to avoid contact with the unknown substance. She tapped in 911 on her receiver and soon an operator answered.

"911. What is your emergency?" said the operator.

"I have received an envelope in the mail from an unknown person and there is a fine white powder inside. It's on my lap. I don't know what to do," she said, providing the operator with what she thought was a succinct description of the most pertinent pieces of information that police officials would need to know to determine what to do—if anything.

The operator didn't waste any time. She immediately asked for Essie's name and location and assured her that an officer would be there shortly. She also attempted to acquire information as to Essie's response to the powder. Essie assured the operator that she was experiencing no physical symptoms other than fear. The operator continued to ask questions and provide information that Essie realized was designed to calm Essie while giving the police time to arrive.

"Ma'am," asked the operator, "you say you're a resident at Happy Haven Assisted Living Facility?"

"Yes," repeated Essie and once again she gave the operator the address and her room number.

"Is the door to your room open?"

"No," replied Essie, understanding what the operator was attempting to determine. "It's closed but it's not locked. Please just tell whoever comes to come right in."

"Yes, ma'am," said the operator, "please remain where you are. Try not to move around. We have someone on the way."

Essie was gratified that apparently they were taking her problem seriously. She had worried that when the operator discovered that she was an elderly woman in an assisted living facility they would dismiss her concern as frivolous. She carefully lifted her arm in an attempt to check her wrist watch. *How long has it been?* she wondered. Obviously, the police couldn't arrive instantaneously, but it did seem as if quite some time had passed. *Of course*, she reasoned, *when you're sitting in a rigid position with a layer of what might potentially be a deadly poison in your lap, time probably did seem to go by more slowly.*

This would probably all turn out to be nothing. The police would arrive, take one look at the powder, immediately recognize it as some obvious household substance that they dealt with every day, and laugh at her under their breath. That would be fine with her. She'd rather feel foolish than allow any of her friends or any of the staff at Happy Haven to be put in jeopardy.

It had to be a coincidence. Just some simple ingredient that her secret admirer had used to fill the heart. Nothing sinister. She simply didn't know anyone who bore her any ill will and would want to hurt her. Or did she? She thought and thought. Even if there was such a person, why go to all this trouble? Or if it was a terrorist. Someone who was out to hurt anyone. Many people. If so, why go about it in such a convoluted manner? If anyone wanted to terrorize people by sending poison through the mail, surely they would send it to someone who was more in the public eye. And surely they would make the poison more accessible to the victim when they opened the letter. Indeed, if she hadn't been so curious about the creation of this valentine, she might never have discovered the powder inside the little heart. The powder might never have been released. That was surely not what a terrorist would want to do.

The operator was talking to her again. Probably just to make sure she was still there and hadn't succumbed to the effects of the poison. If the stuff on her lap was poison, it obviously wasn't a quick-acting type. Essie didn't feel the least bit ill. It was probably truly some sort of salt. She lifted her knee slightly because her rigid position was becoming very uncomfortable. The powder again puffed up into the air. She could see little clouds of it drift off towards her window. *Great,* she thought. *Oh well, better than towards my nose.*

"Miss Cobb," she heard the operator say from the receiver that she had put down. "Are you still there, Miss Cobb?"

She picked up the phone and spoke into it.

"I'm here," she replied. "It's just hard to sit so still. I'm trying not to move around. Every time I do, this stuff flies up in the air."

"We understand, Miss Cobb," replied the operator calmly. "It won't be long. We have officers on the way."

At that moment, there was a knock on her door.

"Yes?" she called out.

"Miss Cobb!" came a voice from outside. "It's the police."

"The door is open. Please come in," Essie replied with tremendous relief.

The door opened slowly and a man's head peeked inside. He glanced around the room, his eyes focusing on Essie seated on her recliner. He motioned to someone behind him and quickly and quietly, the man and a woman officer entered Essie's apartment. The female officer gently closed the door behind her.

The man came over to Essie and the woman remained behind, apparently guarding the door.

"Miss Cobb," he said. "What's this about a powdery substance you received in the mail?"

Essie pointed down at her lap, her shoulders dropping in relief.

Chapter Thirteen

"Love and marriage go together like angel cake and anthrax."

—Julie Burchill

"I'm Officer Magee and this is Officer Chavez," he said. "Do you mind if I take a closer look at this stuff?"

Essie shook her head, her heart pounding as the man kneeled down beside her and stared at the heart she was clutching in her hand and the little rivulet of powder that had dribbled down onto her trousers.

"Hmmm," he said, staring at the powder while he balanced precariously in his bended position. He obviously was attempting to get as close as possible without actually touching the powder or Essie. He stood up and walked over to the female officer at the door. They whispered a bit. Essie couldn't make out what they were saying, but soon the man returned and pulled a pair of rubber gloves out of his pocket. He also extracted a small, blue, plastic face mask, the kind Essie had seen medical people wear sometimes when she went to her doctor's office. He slipped the mask over his face.

"Just a precaution, Miss Cobb," he said warmly. He bent down again and reached out and carefully took the tiny heart that Essie was clutching with such force that even she did not realize how firmly she had it in her hands. "It's okay, Miss Cobb. I've got it. You can let go." Essie slowly released her fingers from around the heart. Officer Magee reached into his back pocket with his free hand and brought out a large, clear plastic envelope, like the kind the dining hall sometimes put sandwiches in for Saturday night picnic dinners. He carefully slipped the heart into the baggie, being cautious not to allow any more powder to fall onto Essie. Then he rubbed the top of the bag together and it made an audible snap, closing securely.

"I'm not really certain what we should do about all this powder on your lap. I'm afraid if I try to scoop it up, it will just disperse even more. I'm thinking we'd better just have you stay seated like this and not move until we get some idea of what we're dealing with."

"Okay," replied Essie in a hoarse voice. She felt a certain amount of relief now that someone was there who seemed to know what they were doing and who evidently had the resources to do something. However, there was still powder on her lap and that was causing her a great deal of anguish.

Magee placed the baggie with the powder-filled heart in a manila envelope that Chavez pulled from a clipboard she was holding under her arm.

"Get this over to the lab, Chavez," he said to the woman. "Asap." Chavez nodded and slipped the envelope under the clip on her board and quietly exited Essie's room.

"I'm going to stay here with you, Miss Cobb," he replied. "Just in case."

Essie knew his unstated message was "just in case this is poison and you've been exposed." She tuned in to her bodily functions. Her breathing seemed unusually fast, but that could be from all the excitement. She didn't seem to be experiencing any other physical symptoms.

As if he was reading her mind, Magee asked, "Are you feeling okay, Miss Cobb?"

"I think so," she said.

"Can you hold on just a bit?" he asked. "I'm going to call headquarters and see what they want to do about this. Obviously, we can't leave you sitting here indefinitely with all this...stuff...all over you." He smiled warmly at her, but then gave her a serious glare as if to say, *don't move*.

"Yes," she said. "I'm used to sitting here in my recliner."

"Good!" he replied, rising. He moved over to the window and looked out while he pulled out a cell phone and quickly called a number. Essie couldn't hear his whispered conversation, but she did gather that he was attempting to convey some urgency. Every so often, Magee would turn and look at her, sitting, she imagined rather forlornly, in her chair. Then he turned back and responded to the voice on the phone. She caught several words—strange powder, unknown sender, fine, white—were some that she recognized. Finally, Magee finished the call and returned to Essie. He sat cautiously on the edge of the sofa next to her.

"Miss Cobb," he began.

"Call me Essie," Essie said.

"Essie," he said. "Can you tell me about this powder? Do you know who sent it?"

"I got it in the mail yesterday," she explained. "It was in this beautiful valentine from a secret admirer." She pointed to the card on the end table between her and the policeman. He reached over cautiously and picked up the card, his hands still wearing the rubber gloves.

"Wow!" he said with a whistle. "This is some fancy card!"

"I know," said Essie. "I was flattered, but mystified. I tried to figure out who might have sent it but I couldn't. My friends all tried to help me figure it out but we simply haven't been able to. My granddaughter is a graphic designer and she thought that the card was made by the person who sent it; she said she didn't think anyone had bought it in a store." Essie explained to the officer how Mindy had convinced her that the card had been created just for her. "Oh, no! Now I've put my granddaughter's health and safety in jeopardy by letting her touch this card!" She felt a wave of anguish shake her entire body and her hands flew to her face before she had even considered the consequences.

"Essie," Magee said quickly, "please don't touch your face! Let's wait and see what our lab finds out about that powder first, okay?"

Essie quickly dropped her hands back to her lap.

"I'm sorry," she replied, sobbing. "I've shown this card all over Happy Haven. If it's poisonous, I've exposed everyone here!"

"Now, let's not jump the gun," said Magee. "We don't know it's poison yet. We're just being cautious."

"But what else could it be?" she cried, as several more tears dripped down her face. She used her shoulder to rub them away.

"You know, Essie," he confided, "this isn't the first mysterious substance case I've seen."

"It isn't?" she asked.

"Nope," replied the young officer with an expressive smile. "Last year, Chavez and I got called out to a house where a young mother found her toddler had gotten outside and had wandered back into the house covered with a blue liquid."

"Oh, no!" cried Essie, now more concerned for a baby she didn't even know than herself.

"Yep," he said, shaking his head. "We thought he might have accidentally gotten into some weed killer in the garage. The mother didn't know where he'd gone. We had to scoop some of that substance off the kid and have it analyzed in the lab. We would have taken the kid to the hospital, but he wasn't showing any adverse symptoms. Luckily, the blue stuff turned out to be some weird flower they had in their garden. The kid decided to eat several of the blossoms. It was totally harmless, just messy. But I tell you, that mother was worried sick. And, boy, did she feel guilty."

"She should have. She let her baby run away and didn't know where he'd gone!" exclaimed Essie.

"Kids are quick!" said Magee, smiling. "I know; I've got one of my own."

"Oh, you're married?" asked Essie.

"For about two years now," replied Magee. "We have a son who just turned one. He's into everything. You really need eyes in the back of your head to keep track of them."

"Oh, I know! I raised three myself!" said Essie.

"And they survived, right?" asked Magee.

"So far," said Essie, now looking down again at her lap and the small streams of white.

Magee quickly turned the topic of conversation in a different direction. He asked Essie about herself and her time living at Happy Haven and she was happy to have the distraction. After quite a while, she had calmed somewhat. Soon, there was a knock on the door and Officer Chavez popped her head inside.

"Hey, Chavez," said Magee from the sofa. "You're back!"

Chavez entered, followed by a man in a long overcoat and hat. Chavez remained by the door, her police jacket still on. The tall man moved over to Magee.

"Detective," said Magee, standing. "This is Miss Cobb, Detective. Essie, this is Detective Abbott." Having made the appropriate introductions, Magee stepped out of the way, and wandered over to the window where his partner was waiting.

"Miss Cobb," said Abbott, "we've just received the report from our lab on your mystery substance here." He looked down at Essie's lap quizzically. "Happy to report, there's no poison. None at all!"

Essie felt a gigantic rush of relief course through her body. Not only was she safe, but her friends at Happy Haven and her granddaughter and any other person who may have been exposed were also safe.

"Oh, my!" she cried. "I'm so relieved! Thank you, Detective!"

"You're welcome, Miss Cobb," replied the detective. "We take tampering with the U.S. mail very seriously. And we certainly don't like the idea of anyone taking advantage of our senior citizens—such as yourself."

"You really did that quickly!" said Essie.

"We've got a good lab," he said.

"I guess I can just brush this stuff off of my lap then," she said. "I've been a virtual prisoner of my chair since I spilled it." She bent forward as she started to get up and out of her recliner.

"Um, just a minute, Miss Cobb," said the detective, holding up a hand. "Not so fast."

"What?" she asked, freezing in place.

"It's true the lab tested the powder and cleared it as any type of poisonous substance. But that's not the end of it."

Magee and Chavez looked intently at Abbott as he spoke. They both moved closer. Essie was riveted in her recliner as the big man with the thick brown hair suddenly became the focus of attention in Essie's small apartment.

"The lab discovered something else about this substance of yours," said Abbott, staring at Essie.

"They did?" she asked.

"Yes," he said. "Luckily, the lab is very thorough in its testing. They not only checked this substance to be certain that it wasn't poison. They also checked to determine what it was."

"And what is it?" asked Essie, totally mystified.

"Cocaine," replied Abbott.

The room was silent. Chavez and Magee exchanged glances. Essie felt as if she had been slapped in the face.

"What?" she asked.

"Yes," he said, towering over her. "High grade cocaine, ready for distribution. This small amount in your little heart here would probably reap about $5,000 for a dealer on the open market. Not a fortune, but this stuff isn't just beach sand either."

"I don't understand," said Essie. "Why would anyone send me $5,000 worth of cocaine? I don't use drugs. I don't know anyone who uses drugs. Except, of course, those that are approved by Medicare."

"That's definitely something we intend to find out," said Abbott. "That card you say this stuff was in? Where is it? Do you have the envelope it came in?"

Essie picked up the card and envelope and handed them to the detective.

"Chavez," he said, holding the card and envelope by the edges. Chavez came over with another plastic evidence bag and Abbott dropped the card and envelope into it. "Get this to the lab." Chavez headed out with a nod.

"One thing, Miss Cobb," Abbott said when Chavez had disappeared. "You don't need to sit like a statue in that chair anymore. Why don't we get you out of there?"

"Yes, Essie," added Magee, coming over. "You can stand up and we can have you shake off the powder on your lap."

"Just how much is the stuff on my lap worth, do you think?" she asked as they helped her get out of her chair.

"Couple hundred bucks, probably," replied Abbott. The two men cautiously helped Essie shake her clothes and stretch her legs.

"Well, that was an expensive spill, wasn't it?" she sighed.

Chapter Fourteen

"It is impossible to love and to be wise."

—Francis Bacon

After Essie had stretched her legs a bit, Detective Abbott took off his overcoat and laid it carefully over the back of one of Essie's armchairs. He motioned to Magee to stand by the door.

"Miss Cobb," Abbott said, as he sat down on the sofa and bent in towards Essie. "We have some questions for you."

"But Detective," she replied, bewildered, "I don't know anything about cocaine. I had no idea that was an illegal drug in my heart. I just assumed it was some sort of stuffing to give the little heart some shape. And when I actually saw the powder, the first thing I thought of was that anthrax scare from years ago when that maniac sent that poison through the mail. That's why I phoned 911."

"You did exactly the right thing," said Abbott, in an assuring tone. "There was no reason for you to suspect drugs. Actually, we're rather surprised to find it, but it does create a new problem. As you can imagine, the government frowns on people sending illegal drugs through the United States mail. When we discover such a substance being sent this way, we are obviously anxious to find out who sent it. We're also interested in finding out the identity of the intended recipient. Obviously, it wasn't you. You were a ploy."

"What do you mean?" asked Essie, puzzled.

"I mean, you were never the intended recipient of this valentine," replied Abbott, his intense brown eyes unwavering as he looked at Essie.

"But it was sent to me!" she exclaimed.

"Yes," he said. "But you were not really meant to receive it. At least, that's what we think."

"How could that be, Detective?" she asked.

"We suspect that someone probably planned to intercept this card before it ever reached your hands," he explained. He maintained eye contact with Essie as he clenched his hands and cracked his knuckles audibly.

"Wouldn't it be simpler just to send the card to the person who it was intended for in the first place?" she asked.

"Simpler, but not safer," he replied. "If the card ever were intercepted by law enforcement—just as has happened— having your name on the card protects the actual recipient from being exposed."

"I don't understand," said Essie, shaking her head is disbelief. "How would this person even know that I got this card, or when I got this card in the mail?"

"That's a good question," Abbott said. "And it's something we don't know the answer to. But, Miss Cobb, we have reason to believe that the person who sent this card to you is part of a large drug ring that federal agents have been tracking for years. We've been in contact with agents in

Boston—where your card was postmarked—and they believe that your card was sent from a major dealer. Whoever the card was intended for is probably just a minor cog in the machine, but if we could nab this person, he or she might be able to lead us to the major dealer that we know is headquartered in the Boston area."

"From the return address?" she asked.

"Not so much that," he said. "You can write any false address as a return address and this guy knows that, but you can't fake a postmark, and your envelope has a Boston postmark. We know where it came from and when. We need to move fast so we can help law enforcement in the Boston area crack this drug ring."

"I certainly hope you do, Detective," said Essie firmly. "These people have caused me enough anguish."

"We need your help, Miss Cobb," said Abbott, reaching out and grabbing her hand.

"What?" she cried.

"We certainly don't wish to embroil you in anything dangerous, but we doubt that the intended recipient of this cocaine represents any actual threat to you. This is probably someone who has been using this scheme for some time now and needs the residents of Happy Haven to maintain this business. This person just wants the drugs so they can distribute to their users. They're probably just a small-time dealer, a small part of a big organization. But somehow they have managed to involve you in their business. The only way we see to capture them is to use you as bait."

"What?" she cried again. Magee moved closer and sat next to Abbott on the sofa.

"Detective," Magee said. "I had the opportunity to speak with Essie before you arrived and I think you're scaring her. Can you let me try?"

"Sure, Magee," said Abbott with a wave of his arms, rising and moving over to the window.

"Essie," said Magee in a soft voice, bending in to her, "I think what Detective Abbott is asking for is your help in catching a criminal. You were telling me earlier about how you've solved some mysteries here at Happy Haven. What Detective Abbott is asking for is your help in solving another one of those mysteries. Right, Detective?" Magee turned his head and looked over at the window.

"Yup," said Abbott, nodding.

"Essie is a real detective herself," Magee said to Abbott. "She's actually rather famous around here." Abbott listened to Magee list some of Essie's exploits and responded with a shrug. He came back and sat back down on the sofa.

"You can think about all of this as a mystery, Miss Cobb," he said. "We don't know who the intended recipient of your valentine is—and we need to know, if we're going to break up this ring."

"And you think I can help?" she asked.

"We do," replied Magee softly.

"We think you'd be the key to solving this mystery," added Abbott. "So far, we believe we've been fairly discreet in our comings and goings. But just in case, we're going to use a cover story that we want you to use too in case anyone asks why the police were visiting you. Just say that the police came to answer your call for help regarding an insurance phone scam. How does that sound?"

"Fine. I can say that. Do you think this person might hurt me or anyone here at Happy Haven?" she asked cautiously.

"Highly unlikely," said Abbott, again cracking his knuckles. "Whoever this person is, they don't want to jeopardize their set-up here by exposing themselves to you. So, will you help us, Miss Cobb?"

"I guess so," she said. "Will I need a gun?"

The men laughed and smiled at each other.

"No, Essie," said Magee. "No pistol for you."

"What we need from you is information," said Abbott, pulling out a small black notebook and a pencil. "So put your thinking cap on and see what you remember."

"My thinking cap is always on, Detective," Essie said, rolling her eyes. "What do you need to know?"

The two officers proceeded to quiz Essie about the particulars of the card and when she had received it. Essie informed them about all of her movements since the moment she'd pulled the envelope from her mailbox until the moment when she discovered the white powder in the little heart.

"So, you would say that many people here at Happy Haven are aware that you received this valentine?" asked Abbott, ready to note Essie's response in his notebook.

"I can't imagine there's anyone who lives at Happy Haven who hasn't heard about it from me directly or from someone else," she said.

"Hmmm," said Magee, looking over at Abbott.

"And, of course, someone searched my room," added Essie.

"What?" asked Abbott. "You think your room was searched?"

"Yes," replied Essie. "I came back to my apartment and I noticed that things were not in the places they were supposed to be. Nothing was missing."

"You're sure?" asked Magee.

"Oh, I'm sure," said Essie. "It's just that it appeared that someone had moved my things around. I think they were trying to find the valentine, but they couldn't because I had it with me. I've kept it with me ever since I got it. Safe in my walker basket."

The men stared at each other.

"Miss Cobb," said Abbott, "we're going to have someone keep an eye on you. An undercover agent. You won't be aware of the person, but they'll be around if you need them. I don't like the idea of someone searching your room." He cracked his knuckles even louder. Essie surmised that the more worried he became, the louder he cracked.

"I don't either!" said Essie. "I don't like people messing with my things!"

"So," continued Abbott, "we want you to just go about your daily activities as if nothing is different. You can talk about the valentine if you want to but obviously, don't mention calling us."

"But you have the card and the envelope now," she said. "Before, I could show it to people. The ladies here really liked seeing it. It was from a secret admirer, you know!" Essie smiled proudly.

"Yes," said Abbott, "a clever ploy on the part of the dealer. If anyone from the Post Office opened the letter, it looked innocuous. "

"You can pretend you have the card," suggested Magee, "even if you don't."

Essie thought about his idea and nodded.

"Hmm," she said. "I guess I can. No one needs to know it's not in my basket anymore. I can still talk about it as if it's there." She reached over to her walker and patted the seat.

"So, Miss Cobb," continued Abbott, laying out his plan, "we want you to just go about your daily routine. Don't do anything different or anything that might draw attention to yourself or to the valentine. We will be keeping an eye on you and if anyone tries to get into your basket, we'll stop them."

"That is very reassuring, Detective," said Essie.

"We will do our part," said Magee, cautiously, "but, Essie, you have to do your part if we're going to catch this person. Don't you take any crazy chances."

"Why would I do that, Officer?" asked Essie.

"Oh, I don't know," he laughed. "I've only known you for a little while, but I already have the feeling that nobody takes advantage of you. You're obviously one smart cookie!"

"I hope you're right," replied Essie. "And I hope that we can work together and catch this drug dealer."

At that, there was a loud knock on Essie's front door.

"Now who?" she moaned. The policemen looked at each other. Abbott nodded to Magee who rose and peeked out the door.

"Essie!" cried both Marjorie and Opal standing in the doorway. Fay was positioned behind them in her wheelchair. Marjorie ignored the man clutching the door and forced it open.

"Where's Essie?" she demanded. The two women rolled their walkers in, followed by Fay in her wheelchair. Magee was almost thrown against Essie's small sink.

"Essie," said Opal when she saw Essie sitting in her recliner. "Are you all right? When you didn't show up for lunch, we all became worried that you might be sick!"

"Or in trouble!" exclaimed Marjorie, glaring back at Magee who was cowering at the sink.

Opal stared at Abbott sitting on Essie's couch.

"Who are these men, Essie?" she demanded.

"You see, Officers," said Essie calmly, speaking to both policemen. "I have a lot of good back-up."

"Officers!" cried Marjorie from the center of the room. "Have you been arrested, Essie? Don't worry! We'll defend you!"

"I haven't been arrested, Marjorie!" replied Essie, arms up in the air. "Calm down."

Abbott rose and motioned for the three women to take seats. He nodded to Magee to shut Essie's front door.

"What is going on?" asked Opal, seated on the small sofa next to Marjorie. Fay wheeled over to the far end of the sofa.

"I'm a special agent!" proclaimed Essie proudly.

Chapter Fifteen

*"Love is not blind—it sees more, not less. But because it sees
more, it is willing to see less."*

—Rabbi Julius Gordon

"Umm," said Abbott, "Miss Cobb, I'm not sure it's advisable
to discuss...."

"Detective," said Essie pointedly to the man who was now
standing. "These women are my three best friends. I share
everything with them. They know all about the valentine.
In fact, they helped me find out most of what I know about
it. There is no way I can keep them in the dark about all of
this."

"All of what, Essie?" asked Marjorie. Opal and Fay also
stared at Essie, expecting a response. Essie looked back at
Abbott, with a pleading expression on her face.

Finally, as the four women scowled at him, he threw up his
arms. "Oh, all right! I guess it's too late to keep them out
of it now!" He moved over to the armchair where his coat
was draped and sat down, scrunching the two stuffed
animals resting on the seat cushion. A deep sigh escaped
his mouth.

Magee remained at the door, an almost imperceptible smile
on his face. It was obvious to Essie that he hadn't seen his
superior in such a disgruntled form before.

As Abbott slunk into Essie's armchair, Marjorie and Opal sat up straighter. Eyeing the man, they quickly turned their attention to Essie.

"What's this about your valentine, Essie?" asked Opal.

"Why are the police interested in a card from your secret admirer?" Marjorie chimed in.

"My, oh my!" cried Essie. "I can't believe this is all happening!"

"Start at the beginning," said Opal.

"Now why should I do that, Opal?" sneered Essie. "If I start at the beginning, it would be a waste of time. You all know what happened from the beginning because I told you all about it. How I got this valentine from a secret admirer. Then you all helped me try to find out who he was."

"Actually, Fay did most of that," noted Marjorie, smiling over at Fay. "If it hadn't been for her, we wouldn't have discovered that the return address on the envelope was fictitious and there was no such place in Boston."

"And don't forget," added Opal, "that Fay found out on the Internet that the company that supposedly made this greeting card didn't exist. That's what led you to begin to think that it was homemade."

"What?" asked Abbott, perking up from his chair. "You ladies actually researched this valentine when you received it?"

"Of course, Detective," said Essie. "Didn't I tell you? Just because we're old doesn't mean we're slow!"

"Who thinks we're slow?" demanded Opal.

"And I told you that my granddaughter Mindy believed that the card was homemade, Detective!" added Essie.

"What were you saying about the company that made the card?" Abbott asked.

"Fay researched it online," said Opal finally, in her authoritative tone.

"And Fay is?" he asked, looking around. The silent lady in the wheelchair raised her hand sheepishly and smiled at Abbott.

"And you found...?" he prompted her.

"Oh, Fay doesn't talk, Detective," interjected Marjorie. "But she knows what's going on, believe me!"

"That's for sure," added Essie, smiling warmly at Fay.

"And what did she find?" Abbott redirected his question to the other women.

"She found that there is no Boston Bell Greeting Card Company," announced Opal, regally. "That was the name in the logo on the back of the card."

"Where is the card, Essie?" asked Marjorie.

"They took it to the lab," replied Essie.

"Why?" asked Opal. "Why do the police care about the identity of your secret admirer?"

"Oh, not because of the secret admirer," replied Essie. "Because of the cocaine!"

"The what?" cried Marjorie.

"Cocaine?" shouted Opal.

"Ladies! Please!" said Abbott in a pronounced whisper. "Keep your voices down!" He looked over at Magee who was still manning the door.

"Why would someone send Essie cocaine?" asked Marjorie. Then, suddenly, her demeanor changed. "Oh, my, Essie! Are you a drug addict?"

"Of course not, Marjorie!" replied Essie, annoyed. "How could you think such a thing?"

"You mean your secret admirer was trying to get you hooked on illegal drugs, Essie?" asked the ever thoughtful Opal.

"No!" cried Essie. "If you all would just be quiet for a minute and let me explain, you'll understand! I didn't know about the cocaine, actually. I was just sitting here in my chair examining the card. I kept thinking that the more I knew about how it was made, the greater the likelihood that I might be able to identify my secret admirer. After all, Mindy did suggest that the card was actually made by the same person who sent it. So, I figured that since my secret admirer made this card, I might learn something about him if I...well...took it apart."

"Oh," said Marjorie softly.

"The little heart," added Opal.

"Yes," said Essie, nodding. "I got out my nail file and I carved open a small opening in the back of the heart and some of the stuffing fell out on my lap. I expected to see sand or salt or foam rubber or something similar. But instead I saw all this very fine, white powder. The only thing that came to mind was...."

"Poison!" exclaimed Marjorie.

"You mean you thought someone had sent poison to you in the mail?" asked Opal. "That seems a little far-fetched."

"Well, what would you have thought, Opal, if all this white stuff had puffed out onto you? It's one thing to chastise me now, but I bet if it was you and you were all alone, you would have thought the same thing." Essie puffed out her cheeks and crossed her arms in annoyance.

"Now, ladies," said Abbott. "It doesn't really matter what Miss Cobb was thinking or what you...Miss Opal...might have done. What matters is what actually happened. And that Miss Cobb called us. And lucky that she did. If she hadn't, we would not have discovered the cocaine in this card and this drug ring would continue on unabated."

"Drug ring?" asked Marjorie. "You mean a drug ring here at Happy Haven?"

"At least a part of it," replied Abbott. "We believe the hub is located in Boston."

"See!" cried Marjorie. "That's where your envelope was sent from, Essie!"

"I know, Marjorie," replied Essie. "It's postmarked Boston."

"Maybe now the police can figure out that indecipherable return address," suggested Opal.

"No," said Abbott. "That return address is indecipherable for a reason. The sender doesn't want anyone to decipher it."

"I understand, Detective," said Marjorie. "But I still don't understand why this drug dealer in Boston sent this cocaine to Essie. Essie may be a little weird..."

"Really, Marjorie!" cried Essie.

"Well, you are unusual, Essie," replied Marjorie. "Even you would have to agree with that!"

"I'm not a drug addict!" exclaimed Essie. Opal lifted a finger as if she had an idea. "And I'm not a drug dealer either, Opal! Really! I would think my three best friends would have more faith in me!"

"If it's any help," noted Abbott, still in the center of the room, seemingly trying to manage the flow of information and at the same time extract any additional information, "we don't suspect Miss Cobb...Essie...of any involvement in this drug ring at all."

"There!" cried Essie. "I hope that clears it up for you, Marjorie!"

"Why me?" asked Marjorie, flouncing. "Opal was just as curious as I was!"

"Never mind," said Essie. "As it is, I wouldn't have any idea what to do with cocaine even if I did recognize it on my lap."

"I think you snort it," suggested Opal.

"I don't want to know what to do with it, Opal!" replied Essie.

"No," offered Marjorie. "I think you put it in a teaspoon and hold it over a flame and then drink it!"

"I don't care!" cried Essie. "Detective! Please! Can you talk to them?"

"Yes," said Abbott. "Let's all sit down!" He grabbed a straight back chair from Essie's desk and set it in the middle of the room. The women took their seats. Abbott straddled the chair so he could see all four women easily. The women watched him and waited.

"Now, ladies," he said. "I wasn't going to bring anyone else into this except Miss Essie. Obviously, she's already involved so we can't really keep her out. I was hoping not to involve any other residents here at Happy Haven, but it's clear that the four of you are all very close..."

"Humph!" snorted Essie, still peeved at Marjorie.

"And not only close, but it appears that all four of you are as involved in Miss Essie's secret admirer valentine as she is. Just before you arrived, I was explaining to Miss Essie how we wanted her to help us catch this person here at Happy

Haven who is apparently involved with this Boston-based drug ring. She has agreed to help and I hope the rest of you will also agree to assist us. Will you?"

The women looked at each other and then quickly nodded in unison.

"Wonderful!" he said. "Now..."

"Detective," said Opal, interrupting his speech. "Why do you think this drug dealer sent this card to Essie? Why didn't he just send it to the drug dealer?"

"As I've already explained to Essie," said Abbott, "her name is being used as a cover for protection in case the Post Office should become suspicious and open the card. If the true recipient's name were placed on the card, yes, it would get to the person faster, but with much greater risk. This way, the drug dealer here at Happy Haven has some way of knowing that the Boston dealer is going to be sending the cocaine to Essie on a certain day and he or she makes arrangements to intercept it before Essie receives It. In this case, he wasn't successful."

"That's why he broke into my apartment and searched for it yesterday!" said Essie.

"He did?" asked Opal. "Did you catch him?"

"No," said Essie, "but I know someone was here. And if he was looking for the valentine, he wouldn't have found it because..."

"Because you always keep it in your walker basket!" said Marjorie, finishing her sentence.

"Right!" noted Essie.

"All of this supports our suspicions," declared Abbott. "If you ladies have any other information that would apply to the valentine we would love to hear it."

"What about Betsy?" asked Opal, tapping her forehead.

"Betsy?" asked Abbott.

"Oh, my!" cried Essie. "I forgot about Betsy!"

"Who is Betsy?" asked Abbott a second time.

"Betsy Rollingford," said Essie. "She got a valentine from a secret admirer last year. We talked about our cards and from everything she told me, her card was almost identical to mine."

"We may want to speak with Betsy and look at her card," said Abbott, noting the woman's name in his black notebook.

"That's impossible!" said Essie. "She displayed her card on her television set when she got it and a day or so later, it was gone! She told me she looked everywhere for it and asked all over but she never found it."

"Does anyone know this Betsy's room number?" asked Abbott.

"Yes," said Essie because she had learned where the woman's room was after their discussion at Bingo. She provided the number and Abbott directed Magee to quickly go and see if he could have Betsy Rollingford join the group that had already gathered in Essie's apartment.

"It might be a good idea," suggested Essie, "if I give her a call and warn her you're on the way. It might be pretty frightening to have a policeman just appear at your door! Unless you're me, of course!"

Abbott gave permission and Essie made a brief phone call.

Chapter Sixteen

"Some cupids kill with arrows, some with traps"

—Shakespeare

Not long after, Betsy Rollingford joined the group. She sat demurely on the armchair next to Detective Abbott and across from the sofa where Marjorie and Opal were entrenched.

"Miss Rollingford," Abbott began after all the introductions had been made. "Miss Essie tells me that you received a valentine from a secret admirer last year."

"I did, Detective," said Betsy with an unexpected perkiness. "Have you found it?"

"What?" asked Abbott.

"Have you found my valentine?" asked Betsy. "It was stolen soon after I received it. I told Essie about it and now I see she's brought in the police. I can only assume she reported it missing and you gentlemen are hot on the trail. So, have you found it?" Betsy sat primly on the edge of the chair, her hands folded in her lap.

"Um, no, we haven't," replied Abbott, looking back awkwardly at Magee who remained at the door. Magee gave him a shrug.

"Well, then, what's this all about?" asked Betsy with a little punch of her hands on her lap.

"Actually, Miss Rollingford," said Abbott, "we asked you down here because Miss Essie told us that you had received a valentine similar to the one she received."

"Yes," said Betsy, "that is true. Essie showed me her card at Bingo and it looked very much like the one I received."

"Did your card have a little heart on it like Essie's?" asked Abbott.

"Oh, yes!" replied Betsy. "But mine was red, not pink like Essie's. But it was very much the same size as Essie's—at least from the short look I got. Isn't it amazing that we both have secret admirers and that they both sent us such similar cards?" She giggled girlishly.

"You didn't ever have the opportunity to look inside the heart on your card, did you, Miss Rollingford?" asked Abbott.

"No," said Betsy. "Why would I want to do that? Even if I did, it was gone so soon after I put it up on my television. I thought it was a wonderful place to display it; I could see it every time I watched *Wheel of Fortune.*"

"Do you have any idea who took it?" asked Abbott. "Do you remember seeing anyone—one of the staff, another resident, a maintenance worker—anyone who seemed particularly interested in your card?"

"No," said Betsy, placing her hand against her forehead. "I just remember that it was gone soon after I put it up on my TV."

"And you don't know anyone who might have sent you this card? Someone from Boston?" he continued hammering away.

"No, Detective," repeated Betsy firmly. "It was from my secret admirer. If I knew who he was, I would tell you. Besides, it's more romantic not to know, don't you think?"

"Yes, ma'am," replied Abbott, again with a glance at Magee who remained speechless at the door.

Abbott looked up and away from Betsy Rollingford and directed his attention to all of the women in the room.

"Have any of you other ladies every received a valentine, or a greeting card of any sort from a secret admirer? Or, more particularly, have you ever received any type of correspondence that might have included some sort of object that might have been filled with a substance as were these hearts in these two valentines?"

"Substance?" asked Betsy suddenly. "What are you talking about?"

"Essie's heart was full of cocaine," announced Marjorie to Betsy.

"Oh, no!" Betsy cried. "You think my card had cocaine in it too?"

"Of course he does, Betsy!" said Marjorie. "That's why he brought you down here and asked you all those questions."

"Now, ladies," said Abbott, standing as intense discussion broke out among the women. Betsy seemed furious and frightened and the other women all attempted to calm her at the same time. "Please, ladies! Let's all sit back down and discuss this calmly." When silence had settled, Abbott resumed his seat. Magee chuckled to himself.

"Detective," Betsy said, "you think that my secret admirer sent me drugs?"

"Not you, Miss Rollingford," said Abbott. "We believe that these 'secret admirers' are actually a drug ring leader in Boston. We've been in contact with the Boston Police and we're attempting to help them identify this individual by first identifying the intended recipient of these valentines here at Happy Haven."

"He thinks it's someone here," said Essie.

"Like one of the staff or a kitchen worker," added Opal.

"Or even a resident," said Marjorie.

"I can't believe a resident would be a drug kingpin, Marjorie!" snarled Essie. "It's probably some outside worker. One of those men who come in to do the regular bug spraying or fix the heating. They're always going in and out of our apartments. A lot of them look real seedy. They look like drug lords."

"And what does a drug lord look like, Essie?" asked Opal with her knowing look.

"Like any of the men who wander in and out of our rooms, Opal," replied Essie. "They could grab something from one of our apartments and we'd never be the wiser."

"Ladies!" said Abbott, again raising his arms in an attempt to achieve order. "That's what we're trying to determine. That's why we need your help. All of your help." He looked around pointedly from one woman to another.

"What do you want us to do, Detective?" asked Marjorie, smiling flirtatiously at Detective Abbott, her shoulder flounce particularly noticeable.

"Several things," said Abbott. "First, and foremost, don't do anything to endanger yourselves. If you even suspect anything or anyone, I want you to contact me directly." At this point, he handed each woman a business card. "That's my direct line. Call me if you see anything that concerns you."

"Oh, I will," said Marjorie, shoulders gyrating.

"Second," said Abbott, obviously ignoring Marjorie's attempts at seduction, "if anyone should ask about the presence of the police, the cover story is as we discussed. Miss Essie contacted us because she was being harassed by a telephone scammer. That should explain our presence in her apartment. If anyone asks about the rest of you, you can say you were just here to give Miss Essie moral support."

"We can do that," said Opal.

"Of course we can," added Betsy. Fay gave a little hand gesture from her wheelchair to indicate that she too was on board with the plan.

"And finally," said Abbott, "don't discuss the whereabouts of your valentine, Miss Essie."

"I don't know its whereabouts!" Essie exclaimed.

"I know," replied Abbott. "We will be testing it in our lab and running down any lead we can. We really can't return it. I think it best that you not tell people that you no longer have the card, but on the other hand, I don't want you to tell them that you do have it. It's too dangerous. Of course, he may think you have it, no matter what you say."

"Should I say where I keep it?" Essie asked. "If I say it's in my room, the crook will just wait until I'm out of my room to go look for it and then I'll never find out who it is. If I say I have it in my basket, he'll know he won't have a chance to get it because I always keep my walker with me."

"Truthfully, Miss Essie," said Abbott, "I wouldn't do much advertising of where the card is or isn't. I'd just play it coy, if you know what I mean."

"Not really," scoffed Essie. "I usually say what I mean."

"But now, Miss Essie," said Abbott with a flourish, "you're going to have to do some acting—if you want to help us catch this rascal!"

"Oh, she does, Detective!" said Marjorie, beaming.

"We can do this," said Opal, seriously looking from one friend to another. "We just continue our lives as normal. If someone asks about Essie's card, we say we really don't know where it is—and we really don't know where it is. If someone asks you, Essie, you can say it's in a safe place— and it is in a safe place. You just don't have to tell anyone that that safe place is the police lab."

"That makes sense," said Essie, reflecting on Opal's sensible reasoning.

"It does," said Abbott. "How does that sound to the rest of you?" The remaining women nodded their agreement.

With the strategy devised, the women seemingly all breathed a sigh of relief. Abbott and Magee bid the five farewell with a final reminder of the importance of keeping in touch. Abbott also told them that an undercover police officer would be keeping an eye on them in case they ran into an emergency. When the policemen had departed, the women broke out into a riotous conversation.

"This is the most exciting thing that's ever happened at Happy Haven," announced Marjorie.

"Not to me," noted Betsy Rollingford. "I just wanted my valentine back." She pouted but remained seated.

"You're all being ridiculous," said Opal. "We need to snap out of this! Nothing has changed. There is a slight possibility that we might have an opportunity to aid the police in apprehending a criminal—but that possibility is remote, so I suggest we just go about our business and forget entirely about this little episode."

"Opal," cried Essie. "You can forget it if you like! But this drug dealer and his little cocaine-filled valentine has wreaked havoc on my life. I sat in this chair for hours with that foul powder drenching my trousers, not knowing whether or not I'd be dead before the police managed to get to my door, not knowing whether I had exposed my darling granddaughter to the horrible stuff, not knowing whether I had exposed you, and Marjorie, and Fay, and all my other friends here at Happy Haven to some horrible poison! I can't just forget it! And I'm not going to forget it. I'm going to find this creature that did this to me and to all of us!"

"And how do you plan to do that, Essie?" asked Opal.

"I'm not going to play coy like Detective Abbott suggests, that's for sure!" she declared. "If the only way to catch this drug dealer is to lure him into grabbing my valentine, then, by glory goose bumps, I'm going to have a valentine for him to steal!"

"Essie," gasped Betsy, "that sounds very dangerous!"

"Very risky!" added Marjorie.

"Not only am I going to have a valentine for our friendly drug dealer to swipe," noted Essie, now in full plotting mode, "but I'm going to spread the word all around Happy Haven. That valentine is going to go everywhere with me in my basket. If that drug guy wants it, he'll have to come rip it out of my walker seat!"

"No, Essie!" said Opal. "This is foolish talk!"

"Foolish, maybe, Opal," said Essie, "but I've been pushed to it. These drug people picked the wrong person when they sent that secret admirer valentine to Miss Essie Cobb. I will not just sit around meekly and wait for the police to tumble to our culprit. I'm going to get him myself!"

Chapter Seventeen

"Love is an exploding cigar we willingly smoke"

—Lynda Barry

The women did their best to try to talk some sense into Essie, but she was resolute. After promising her friends that she would be careful, the group disbanded, being careful to exit Essie's apartment discreetly, one at a time into an empty hallway.

When she was finally alone, Essie was attacked not by fear but by hunger. She suddenly realized that during the hubbub with the police and her friends' arrival, she had missed lunch in the dining hall. Her stomach was now growling ferociously and it was still hours before dinner.

She rolled over to her small kitchen to see if there was anything in her refrigerator that she could munch on. Inside she saw mostly empty shelves. There was a shriveled up apple in the fruit bin. *I'd better get rid of that,* she thought. Far in the back on the lowest shelf she saw a package of something wrapped neatly in aluminum foil. *Now how long has that been in there?* she wondered. As Essie virtually never ate anything in her own room and always ate her meals in the dining hall, it was a miracle that there was anything in her refrigerator at all. She closed the door in annoyance and reached up over the handle bars of her walker to the cupboard doors. On the middle shelf, she found an old box of cereal. Reading the label, she discovered that this brand included nuts.

"Super squirrels! Nuts!" she cried. "Nuts are protein. Just what I need." She ripped open the top of the box and reached inside for a handful. Gulping down the flakes and tiny nut bits, she soon felt the gnawing in her stomach subside. She grabbed her water glass from the sink and swallowed a full glass of water to wash it all down.

"Probably the quickest lunch I've ever consumed," she said aloud. "This will certainly make me appreciate the food in the dining hall more." Feeling full, she made a quick stop in her bathroom before heading out into the Happy Haven hallway. She realized that she hadn't given a great deal of thought as to how she would handle it, but she felt it was important to make clear to her fellow residents and to the staff that nothing had changed; she still had the valentine, and she was excited to learn who her secret admirer was.

She pushed her walker down the hallway, through the family room, and into the lobby. It was early afternoon and Happy Haven was busy with residents and guests milling about. Phyllis was manning the front desk as usual. Several other staff members, including Sue Barber and Violet Hendrickson, were behind the desk looking through files in the small office immediately behind the front desk. Two men entered the main door carrying a sofa. Essie assumed that either one of the residents had ordered new furniture or someone was moving in. When someone moved in, it typically meant that a resident had moved out. That also typically meant that a resident had died. Essie hadn't heard through the grapevine that anyone had passed away recently so she was curious who the sofa belonged to.

A group of card players in the family room laughed and caught her attention. Essie moved closer to the front desk. Several residents were lined up, probably waiting to sign out or in. Essie waited her turn.

"Essie!" said Phyllis. "I haven't seen you all day! What were those police officers doing in your apartment earlier?" Phyllis asked the question Essie was dreading and the one she had been preparing for even though Phyllis didn't seem that curious about it.

"Oh, that," replied Essie as casually as possible. "I've been getting some annoying phone calls. The police were out to talk to me about them. It appears those calls are part of some widespread senior scam going on around the country. Those idiots tried to sell me land in Florida!" She shrugged her shoulders as if to say her problem was just the tip of the iceberg.

"Oh, no!" replied Phyllis, fumbling though a pile of cards she was sorting. "I hope they didn't take any of your money?"

"No, joe!" said Essie with a little punch of her fist. "I'm too smart for that!"

"I bet you are, Essie!" replied Phyllis, smiling warmly. "What about that secret admirer of yours?" she asked suddenly. "Did you ever find out who he was?"

"Not yet," said Essie in a louder voice. Phyllis had now tackled the subject that truly interested Essie and she was happy to plant the information that she was sure would be heard by other residents and staff and spread as gossip around Happy Haven in no time flat. "But I'm trying to find

out who he is! After all, he sent me such a beautiful
valentine!"

"I heard about that card, Essie!" exclaimed Phyllis, setting
down her work. "I'd love to see it!"

"Oh, show her, Miss Essie!" said Sue Barber from further
back behind the front desk. "It's really beautiful!"

"I'd like to see it too!" added Violet Hendrickson, standing
next to Sue. She gave Essie a warm smile, a totally
unexpected gesture from the otherwise imposing Happy
Haven director.

"Oh, sorry, Phyllis," replied Essie, "I'm late for
a...a...meeting right now. Don't have time to show it to
you!" She quickly pushed her walker away from the front
desk and back into the family room. Phyllis shrugged her
shoulders to the two other staff women and returned to her
file counting.

Essie plopped herself down in a large armchair, out of view
of the front desk.

"I handled that well," she said. Unfortunately, she realized
that it would be a difficult juggling act to indicate to the
people she encountered that she still had the valentine
tucked away in her walker and then not take it out and
show it to them. She'd probably need some sort of valid
excuse that would explain why she claimed to have the card
but was unwilling to show it. She sat lost in thought, the
wheels on her walker rolling slightly back and forth in
reflection of her thought process.

She looked up just in time to see Santos go whizzing through the lobby carrying a covered food tray. The young man headed down her hallway. From where she was sitting, Essie could follow Santos with her eyes all the way to the end of the hallway. As he had done earlier in the day, Santos turned left when he reached the end of the corridor.

Hmm, thought Essie. *I wonder if he's going back to Grace Bloom's apartment again. Why would he be taking her a tray of food when she obviously isn't ill?* Essie's thought were suddenly drawn from attempting to devise the appropriate retort when anyone asked about her secret admirer valentine to trying to figure out why Grace Bloom was getting an invalid's treatment from Santos.

She remained seated but kept her eyes focused on her hallway. This was a good time to be quiet and see what might happen. Her eyes were frozen on the hallway, waiting for either Santos to return with an empty tray or Grace Bloom to appear. She stayed that way, looking down her own hallway for a long time but neither of the two individuals showed themselves. What could be going on? Surely there wasn't anything romantic occurring. Grace was at least eighty and Santos must be no older than thirty. Besides, Essie knew that he had a girlfriend about whom she and her tablemates had heard a great deal. No, it couldn't be anything so salacious. She didn't dare go to Grace's apartment and knock on her door as she had the day before. If Santos was there or if he wasn't, Grace would be more than suspicious of Essie showing up for a second day in a row. No, she'd have to figure out this mystery on her own.

As she sat there contemplating her possible actions, Sue Barber and Violet Hendrickson walked through the lobby and the family room and down the far hallway that led to the chapel, the beauty parlor, and several other locations at Happy Haven.

"Essie!" exclaimed Sue as she almost tripped over her. "I didn't see you there!"

"Sorry, Miss Barber!" said Essie, pulling her walker closer and tucking her feet under the chair.

"Oh, don't be!" replied Sue. "I should watch where I'm going!" She smiled at Essie, and then motioned to Violet and the two women continued down the far hallway. Violet gave Essie a long, expressionless glance as she passed.

That woman gives me the creeps, thought Essie. Essie always tried to stay out of Violet's way. The Happy Haven director seemed to enjoy flaunting her authority and tended to make the elderly residents often feel more like misbehaving children in an elementary school than responsible adults. *After all,* reasoned Essie, *I pay good money to live here. I don't expect to be treated like an inmate. Oh, well, she's only one person.* The rest of the staff were exceptionally pleasant and helpful and Essie loved her three friends, Opal, Marjorie, and Fay.

The diversion of the two staff members passing her caused Essie to lose track of her observation of her hallway. Where was Santos? It had been quite some time since he'd gone down there with that tray. How long did it take to deliver food to someone? This was certainly a mystery. Not the major mystery of the identity of her secret admirer and his intended recipient, slash Happy Haven drug dealer, but a mystery just the same. *My, oh purty pie!* she thought. *I'm really becoming a detective. Two mysteries to solve. I'd better get busy, because so far I haven't had much success at all in solving either.*

Sue Barber and Violet Hendrickson returned down the far hallway off the family room, apparently returning to the front desk or to their offices which were directly off the main entrance, next to the dining hall. They moved past Essie without comment, both smiling politely at her. Essie returned their courteous gesture as she followed them with her eyes back to the lobby. Then she returned her concern to her own hallway. People were going up and down the corridor, but so far neither Santos nor Grace Bloom had made an appearance.

This is ridiculous! Essie thought. *I could wait here all day for one of them to appear.* Grace could just stay in her room indefinitely and maybe Santos left the building through a back entrance. She realized there were other ways to enter and exit Happy Haven besides the main entrance, but residents were required to sign in and out whenever they left the facilities. Maybe Santos had returned to the kitchen through some back hallway of which she wasn't even aware. Well, she'd find out at dinner. She resolved to figure out another way to determine what was going on with Grace Bloom and Santos. She wasn't going to just sit in this out of the way chair indefinitely.

She stood up and rolled her walker into the family room. The group of card players she had heard earlier was still going strong. As she moved closer to them, she recognized several of the members.

"Essie!" called out Dave Esperti. He waved at her then looked back down at his cards and scowled.

Essie rolled over to the table. Here was an opportunity to test her valentine story and spread the word that she still had the card in her possession.

Chapter Eighteen

"Love is that delightful interval between meeting a girl and discovering that she looks like a haddock."

—John Barrymore

"Hey, Essie!" said Dave as she pushed herself over to the corner of the card table, greeting all four players in the process. In addition to Dave, the others included Hubert Darby, Betsy Rollingford, and one other woman Essie didn't recognize.

"Hello," said Essie warmly to the group.

"How's my girl?" asked Dave, patting Essie affectionately on the elbow.

"I'm not your girl," responded Essie lightly, glancing over at Hubert. She knew that Hubert fancied himself her boyfriend and as his romantic gestures were harmless she never really discouraged him. Besides, Hubert was so shy that she wanted to give him confidence when she could. Dave was a different story. He didn't lack any confidence that Essie could tell.

"Oh, saving your heart for that secret admirer, I see!" said Dave broadly for the group. Hubert snorted and looked down at his cards. Betsy also concentrated on her hand. Apparently she hadn't revealed anything to this group about the excitement with the cocaine and the police.

"A secret admirer!" cried the fourth card player. "My goodness! How exciting! Do you have any idea who he is?"

"No," replied Essie to the woman. "But he did send me a beautiful valentine!" She emphasized this last part to make certain that this woman had all the information she needed to spread the word about Essie's card. The more gossip out there, the more likely it would be that the originally intended recipient would hear of it and attempt to get it back.

"I'm Nadine Montrose," the woman said, reaching out and shaking hands with Essie.

"Essie Cobb," replied Essie.

"Didn't you get a card from a secret admirer last year, Betsy?" asked Nadine.

"Umm," said Betsy, obviously not anxious to become involved in the discussion. "Yes, I did, but it was stolen soon after I got it."

"Oh, no!" cried Nadine. "How terrible! Essie, you'd better hang on to yours in case someone Is out there swiping Valentine 's Day cards!" She giggled at her cleverness, and Essie smiled at her sweetly. She didn't realize how true her warning was. "Can we see it, Essie? Your card, I mean."

"Oh, I really don't..." Essie mumbled. She was flustered as she tried to contemplate a reasonable excuse for not showing the card.

"Now, Nadine," said Betsy, leaping into the conversation all of a sudden. "This is a personal matter. Essie received this card from a man. It probably has a very private message on it. She probably doesn't want to share this very private moment with everyone here at Happy Haven." Betsy emphasized "private" and "personal" as she chastised Nadine for asking to view the card.

Essie mentally thanked Betsy for her help in deflecting attention from the now non-existent valentine.

"Hey, Essie," said Dave, "If you don't really want to show us your super private valentine, from that super secret admirer of yours, maybe it's because he's not real."

"What?" asked Essie. Had Dave Esperti figured out her ploy? She didn't think she was doing that badly in covering her attempts to convey information about the card and the fact that she still had it.

"I said maybe your secret admirer isn't real," he repeated pointedly.

"He's real, Dave," said Essie. "Just because I don't want to wave my valentine all around Happy Haven doesn't mean I don't have it and it doesn't exist!" *Now, Essie*, she thought to herself, *don't overdo it*.

"Did you really get a valentine from a secret admirer, Miss Essie?" asked Hubert Darby, looking up at Essie suddenly, his big eyes drooping soulfully. It appeared that he hadn't heard the recent conversation or didn't believe it. Essie glanced from his sad face to that of the face of the spirited Dave Esperti. Why and how did she get herself in these pickles?

"Gentlemen," said Betsy to the men at the table, "really, I do declare! You are both putting Essie on the spot! It's not polite to press a lady about her gentlemen callers like this." Betsy gave stern glances to both Hubert and Dave. The two

men shriveled at her expression and refocused on their
cards.

"Trump!" yelled Nadine suddenly. She laid down a card on
top of one Hubert had just played. With a gleeful smile, she
gathered the trick and placed it on her pile. "You see what
happens when you get involved in conversation and forget
about the game!" Dave scowled and scratched his head.
Hubert sucked on his lower lip and stared at his lap. Betsy
took a deep breath and gave Essie a very brief smile.

"She's right!" added Betsy. "Let's focus on cards and not on
Essie's secret admirer!"

"Would you like to play for me, Essie?" asked Nadine. "I
need to get back to my room. I have a doctor appointment
later today and my daughter will be here to pick me up
shortly."

"That would be lovely," replied Essie, as she scooted herself
into the chair that Nadine was deserting. The two men now
perked up as Essie joined their group.

"So," said Essie. "What game is this?"

"Hearts," answered Hubert and then blushed.

"I like Hearts," replied Essie. Dave dealt a new hand and
Essie quickly joined in the fun. Soon, the four residents
were having a good time, laughing and talking. There was
no more discussion of Essie's secret admirer valentine,
although Essie was certain that the issue hadn't been
forgotten. As the afternoon progressed, Dave and Hubert
seemed to be vying with each other to win Essie's attention
and affection. Essie found the entire enterprise humorous.

The best thing about playing cards with her friends right here in the center of the family room, thought Essie, was that it gave her an excellent view of her hallway. If Santos or Grace Bloom came down the corridor she would be certain to see them.

As it became closer to five o'clock and Essie hadn't seen either of her intended targets come down the hallway, she was beginning to get anxious. Maybe Grace really was ill. Maybe Santos was staying in her room to nurse her. That didn't make sense. Why would a kitchen worker play nurse maid to a resident? Surely, if Grace were ill one of the facility's nurse aides would be there to assist her. What was going on? Essie played a card and ended the latest round of Hearts. Dave and Hubert cried "foul!" Of course, they were only teasing. Essie and Betsy enjoyed rubbing in their victory.

As Essie looked up, she saw Grace Bloom walking briskly down her hallway. The woman did not appear to be sick. She had her cane with her but her pace was even and relatively quick. Grace did not look towards the family room so she did not see Essie sitting at the card table watching her approach. When Grace came into the family room and moved through the lobby, she walked immediately to the dining hall where a line was just beginning to form for the first dinner seating. This must be, she believed, where she had previously seen Grace Bloom. Although Essie always ate during the second seating, she'd probably seen Grace Bloom departing the dining hall at times when she had been lining up for her seating.

The card players were calling it quits for the day. Each resident needed to return to their individual apartments to clean up before dinner. Essie pushed in the chair at the table, rose, and grabbed her walker and started to head back down her hallway. On her way, she rolled around into the lobby where she could see Grace Bloom standing in line. Grace was having a spirited conversation with another woman. Grace did not appear to be sick or upset. *Where is Santos?* wondered Essie. Was he still in Grace's apartment while she was down at dinner? And if so, why? Why would Grace need a kitchen worker to bring her a tray of food when she was going to dinner anyway? Was she that hungry? Grace didn't appear to be inordinately large. Maybe she had some metabolic disease and required more than a normal amount of food. *Oh, that's ridiculous!* thought Essie. There must be a logical reason for this.

I know, she thought. *I'll just make another visit to Grace. If she's not at home—which she obviously isn't—we'll just have to see who answers her door and what explanation they give.* Essie rolled her walker around out of the lobby and back through the family room. She turned right down the corridor that entered her hallway, past her own doorway, and down to the end of her hall. There, she turned left and pushed her vehicle down the carpet, counting the doorways on the left as she went. Five doorways down she read on the door sign, "Grace Bloom." She moved up to the door and gave a short knock.

From inside she could hear lots of muffled noises. There were what appeared to be sounds of scuffling and whispering. *What is going on?* she wondered. She called out. "Grace! Are you there?" She knocked again, but despite the muffled noises that she could definitely hear from deep inside Grace Bloom's apartment, no one came to answer her door.

Tentatively, Essie grabbed the door knob and turned. The door was locked. *Locked! How can that be?* she thought. Virtually no one at Happy Haven locked their doors. If a resident got sick, nurses had to be able to get inside quickly. Yet, there was no doubt. Grace Bloom's apartment door was locked. And despite the fact that someone was apparently inside, no one appeared to be willing to answer the door.

Should she call out to Santos? She thought he might be inside. She had seen him enter this very apartment the day before. She knew that Grace Bloom was presently in line for dinner. She didn't think that Santos—if he was inside— was in any danger. Surely, no danger from Grace Bloom. Whatever was going on, it appeared to be something that they both were involved in. Something that they obviously didn't want anyone else—including her—to know about.

She opted for discretion and turned around and rolled back down the hallway, around the corner and back down to her own apartment. Once inside, and after a quick potty break, she slid comfortably and gratefully into her rocker where she contemplated the various mysteries that had presented themselves to her that day.

Oh, the life of a detective, she thought. *It's a lot of work. Especially when you have more than one case on your plate.* In a few seconds, Essie was sound asleep. Sleep always rejuvenated her. When she awoke, she realized that she would miss dinner if she didn't hurry. *Wonderful*, she thought. *Now I can meet with my three pals and get some help on these mysteries.* There surely must be some logical reasons. Maybe Opal, Marjorie, and Fay had managed to figure out the secret admirer/drug dealer mystery themselves. She pulled herself reluctantly out of her soft recliner and grabbed the handle bars of her walker. With a quick stop in front of her mirror for a face check, she headed out her door and down the hallway to dinner.

Chapter Nineteen

"Speak low, if you speak love."

—Shakespeare

She arrived at the dining hall just after the doors had been opened to allow the group for the second seating to enter. There was Santos, standing at the dining hall door as he always did for the second seating. Had he really been in Grace Bloom's apartment while she was in the dining hall eating dinner? Essie could see Marjorie, Opal, and Fay far ahead in the line. Essie glanced around the room to see if Grace Bloom was still there, but evidently Grace had returned to her apartment.

"Good evening, Miss Essie," said Santos warmly as Essie passed through the doorway.

"Humph," she responded, ignoring the young man who had so skillfully evaded her and her efforts to solve the mystery of Grace Bloom and the food tray. Santos shrugged and smiled at the next resident through the door. Essie rolled over to her table and joined her friends.

"So, Essie," whispered Marjorie, when the four women were seated, "did anyone ask about the valentine?"

"Shhhh, Marjorie," cautioned Essie from the corner of her mouth. "Let's be careful what we say."

"I'm just asking about your valentine, Essie," said Marjorie, pointedly. "You know, the one you received from that secret admirer of yours."

"Yes, yes," responded Essie.

"We thought you were going to talk it up around the building," added Opal.

"Opal," said Essie, "quietly, please. You never know who might be listening." She smiled sweetly at her tablemates and picked up her menu and began to study the evening's entree choices. "Lord's gourds! What a selection!"

Santos appeared at their table with his pad in hand.

"Ladies ready to order?" he asked.

"Oh, Santos!" exclaimed Essie, "you surprised me. You just seem to pop up, don't you?"

Santos laughed uncomfortably.

"I'll have the stuffed peppers," said Opal. Santos recorded her choice and looked up at the other women.

"Oh, me too!" said Marjorie. "They're usually so good!" Santos made a mark on the pad. Fay pointed to the stuffed peppers entree on her menu and Santos added a third mark.

"How about you, Miss Essie?" he asked. "Would you like to join your friends?"

"I don't know," said Essie. "I'm feeling a bit adventurous tonight! Maybe it's because of the beautiful valentine I received from my secret admirer!" She made this announcement in a loud voice so that not only Santos, but all of the surrounding tables and several kitchen workers who were passing heard her remarks.

"That is very romantic," said Santos. "But you are lovely lady, Miss Essie. I can imagine that many of the gentlemen here at Happy Haven have big crush on you." He gave Essie a short bow.

Essie fluffed her hair in a staged gesture of vanity.

"Oh, my admirer isn't from Happy Haven," she announced in her same public address quality voice. "He's from Boston!"

Her three friends grimaced noticeably.

"Boston?" asked Santos. "Boston is very far, is it not?"

"Yes," replied Essie, now sounding as if she were giving a geography lesson. "Boston is located on the east coast in Massachusetts."

"Do you have any idea who this admirer is?" continued Santos, obviously intrigued.

"No," replied Essie, "but I would certainly like to know! It's not every day that a girl has a secret admirer!" She practically yelled the phrase "secret admirer" and directed the comment over her shoulder so that the entire dining hall could hear her remark. "Oh, and Santos, I'll have the oysters!" Her friends gasped, but Santos just chuckled. Having finished collecting the dinner orders from Essie's table, he gave a short bow and swiftly headed back to the kitchen.

"Essie," said Opal in a whisper when the young waiter had retreated, "Oysters! You hate oysters!"

"As do most sensible people," responded Essie, "so I'm sure my ordering them got a lot of attention."

"You aren't being very discreet," said Opal. "And now you'll have to eat those horrid things."

"I'm not that hungry," replied Essie with a shrug.

"You know what Detective Abbott said," added Marjorie, warning her friend.

"Shhh, Marjorie," replied Essie, also in a whisper. "No talk of you know who." She then smiled broadly for the other residents who had taken notice of her. The four women conversed quietly for a while about innocuous topics until the other diners appeared to lose interest in them.

Eventually Santos returned with their dinners.

"How lovely!" exclaimed Opal. "Our chef always does such a nice job with stuffed peppers!"

"He does," agreed Marjorie.

"And oysters for you, Miss Essie," said Santos as he deposited a plate of little brown circles in a buttery sauce in front of her. Essie gulped and smiled politely at the young man. The other women quickly began consuming the peppers which were brimming with finely chopped tomatoes and other fresh vegetables. Essie pushed the oysters around on her plate while she endeavored to ignore the smell of her tablemates' meals. She gingerly stabbed one of the oysters with her fork and took a small bite. After Santos disappeared, the women continued their previous conversation in hushed voices that did not carry to the surrounding diners.

"I hope your overacting did the trick, Essie," noted Opal serenely. "I haven't seen such an over the top performance since the days of silent movies."

"Yes, Essie," added Marjorie, "you're a regular Charlie Chaplin. All that eyebrow raising and arm waving. Aren't you afraid Santos and anyone else watching you order and talk about your secret admirer will become suspicious?"

"And what would they become suspicious of, Marjorie?" asked Essie pointedly.

"That you were lying!" Marjorie replied. "Nobody brags about getting a card with that much gushing. Really!"

"I just wanted to be certain that everyone heard me," said Essie.

"They heard you in Cleveland," said Opal, setting down her fork. She had made short work of her pepper and was now patting her mouth with her napkin.

"The more people who know that I got the secret admirer valentine and that I still have it, the more likely that the intended recipient—the drug dealer," she said, only mouthing this last phrase, "will know where the card—and the cocaine is."

"But you don't have it, Essie," said Marjorie. She too had finished her main course and was waiting for dessert, drinking her coffee.

"Don't remind me, Marjorie," said Essie. "It became painfully evident to me today that it was a problem." Essie was still nibbling on her oyster, as if she were also nibbling on her problem.

"A problem?" asked Opal.

"Yes," said Essie. "It's really hard to talk about this wonderful valentine I received and how much I love it and then not be able to show it to anyone."

"You can't show it if you don't have it," said Marjorie, pointing out the obvious.

"It's at the police lab," added Opal.

"You think I don't know that!" cried Essie in a contained whisper. "Hmm, these oysters aren't half bad." She finished the one on her fork and then speared a second one. "I really wish Detective Abbott hadn't felt the need to take it away. If I had it, it would be so much easier to lure the dealer in to trying to get it."

"Essie!" cried Marjorie. "That's so unwise."

"It's dangerous!" added Opal. "You know what Detective Abbott said about not taking any chances and being discreet. Let the police deal with this. You stay out of it!"

"You two," replied Essie, "have no initiative. The police aren't going to catch this scoundrel. They don't have any way to do it. But I do. I can catch him if I can convince him that I have the card that he wants and he tries to get it."

"And what if he does try to take the card, Essie," noted Opal, "and you get in the way and he...he..."

"What can he do?" asked Essie. "You think this guy would hurt an old lady like me? You think he'd kill me?"

"He might," replied Opal. "You've got his drug supply, or he thinks you do. He may be desperate. He probably isn't going to let you stop him."

"Yes," said Marjorie, "I agree. You are taking a huge chance by flaunting all over Happy Haven that you have that valentine in your possession."

"I don't care," replied Essie. "I'm not going to let him continue to use Happy Haven as his home base and take advantage of my friends here in this drug scheme of his. But without the actual card, I'm forced to pretend that I have it, but that I'm not willing to show it to anyone."

"So?" asked Opal.

"If you were the drug dealer," suggested Essie, "would you believe that I actually had the card if I never showed it to anyone?"

"I might," answered Marjorie.

"That's because you're so gullible, Marjorie," sneered Essie. Marjorie fluffed her blouse and shook her shoulders in her signature move. "If I had the actual card, I could put it on my television just like Betsy did hers and then lie in wait for the dealer to break in and steal it."

"And what if he broke in while you were asleep?" asked Opal.

"I'd stay awake all night," said Essie flippantly.

"Ha!" said Marjorie. "You fall asleep in your chair while watching your shows. You're worse than Fay!" At the mention of her name, the chubby lady in her wheelchair popped awake and looked around at her friends.

"What do you think, Fay?" asked Opal in a confidential whisper. "Should Essie keep up this silly pretense of having the secret admirer card? Even if she is risking her life?"

Fay's eyes bulged out as Opal described the situation. Fay nodded as she listened to Essie's dilemma presented clearly by the group's best analyst. Then she reached across the table and grabbed Essie's hand and squeezed it tightly.

"What does that mean?" asked Marjorie. "Is she giving you her blessing?"

"Of course she is," replied Essie. "Fay is always one for more action and less talk. Right, Fay?"

Fay nodded.

"Really, Fay?" asked Opal. "You think Essie should risk her life by this ridiculous plot that Detective Abbott specifically prohibited?"

Fay stared at Opal and waited for a moment as she appeared to think about the question. She looked at Opal and then over at Essie. All three women focused on their smaller, quieter friend, still clutching Essie's hand. With a final squeeze of Essie's fingers, Fay nodded once.

"See!" said Essie. "Fay agrees with me. You two may be scaredy cats, but I'm not, and neither is Fay. She knows how important this is and she knows that we, or at least I, have a chance to solve this mystery and rid Happy Haven of this drug dealer scourge."

"Oh, all right!" said Marjorie. "I support you! I just hope I don't end up going to your funeral because of this!"

"Me too!" added Opal. "I guess if you're going ahead with this foolish plan, Essie, the least the rest of us can do is have your back."

Santos arrived at that moment with their desserts.

"Ooo!" declared Marjorie, "apple cobbler! I love apple cobbler!"

"Me too!" added Opal. The women suddenly were silent as they dug into the little bowls of fruity, rich goodness.

"Santos," said Essie, as she bit into a large chunk of crispy apple, "I believe I saw you delivering another food tray down my hallway this afternoon. That wouldn't be to Grace Bloom, would it?"

Santos finished placing the last apple cobbler in front of Fay.

"Not remember, Miss Essie. Sorry," he replied and then hastily retreated to the kitchen with their dirty plates.

"What was that about, Essie?" asked Opal. "You asked Santos about delivering food trays earlier. What's going on? Why do you care who he takes a tray to?"

"I know Grace Bloom," added Marjorie. "She's not sick. She was at knitting club this morning."

"She was?" asked Essie, ignoring Opal and focusing on Marjorie.

"Yes," replied Marjorie. "She seemed fine to me. She didn't say anything about needing a food tray. Of course, she didn't stay long either. She only showed up to pick up her knitting project from the last meeting and take it back to her room. I thought that was a bit odd."

"Yes," said Essie. "It was."

"You don't think Grace is involved in this drug dealer scam, do you?" asked Opal suddenly.

"I don't," replied Essie, "but something strange is going on, and I'm not sure what it is. But Santos is usually so open about residents who are having problems. If Grace were ill you'd think he'd let us know so we could help her. Besides, I stopped by her room and she seemed fine, but she surely didn't want me to come in."

"Maybe she's the drug dealer!" offered Marjorie.

"Oh, no!" said Essie. "I can't believe that." And she didn't, but yet she couldn't come up with a reason for the strange goings on between Santos and Grace Bloom.

Chapter Twenty

"I will wear my heart upon my sleeve for daws to peck at."

—Shakespeare

Later that night, as Essie sat in her recliner, waiting for bedtime, she couldn't help but reflect on the events of the day. Now as she sat in her thin pajamas, she felt vulnerable—more vulnerable than she had felt earlier. Then she had been all bravado as she implemented her strategy throughout Happy Haven. By now, surely the entire building was aware of her secret admirer and believed that she had the card in her possession. So far, no one had attempted to take it from her directly, but there was the unknown individual who searched her apartment when she was out. They must have been looking for the card.

Had she done the right thing? She had flagrantly disobeyed the directions of the police who had told her to lay low and be discreet—not something she was known for doing. As she looked around her little apartment, she realized that if the drug dealer was going to come searching for the card, it would very possibly be tonight. Her friends were right. No matter how motivated she was, it would probably be impossible for her to remain awake all night. And when she fell asleep, the culprit would probably sneak into her room, look in her walker basket for the card, and seeing it not there, leave undetected. How would that help to catch him?

There must be a better solution. Essie put on her thinking
cap. Her imaginary thinking cap. It matched her pajamas
well because she often wore it at this time of night.
Logically, she didn't think there was any reason to fear for
her safety because the drug dealer didn't want to reveal his
identity to her and he certainly didn't want to do anything
to upset his little business at Happy Haven. She assumed
that would mean not hurting or frightening any of the
residents, such that the authorities would be called. Of
course, the dealer probably wasn't aware that the
authorities had been called and Essie intended to keep it
that way—at least until she could catch him.

But how? If this fellow sneaked into her apartment and
searched her things and her basket, how would she know
unless she was awake? And, if she was awake, the man
probably wouldn't come in. He'd probably be very careful
not to enter if he had any suspicion that Essie even might be
awake.

Of course, she reasoned, *If he found the valentine, he'd exit
and be satisfied and not bother me anymore.* But then she
wouldn't know who he was. He certainly wasn't going to
stop her in the hallway and thank her for the valentine. Oh,
how she wished she still had that card! The possibilities for
catching the dealer just seemed greater when she
possessed the card. She could show it around. She could
hide it and see who came looking for it. Without the card,
she was forced to act. That is, she was forced to become an
actress and pretend that she had the card when she didn't.
That was really hard for her to do. She'd rather face the
danger of the drug dealer breaking in and stealing the card

from her walker than be constantly pressed to pretend something that didn't exist.

A light bulb went off. Essie felt it as if a little pop exploded right inside her head. It dawned on her that the drug dealer at Happy Haven was expecting a card, probably a valentine, and probably addressed to Essie. What he probably wasn't expecting or didn't know was what that valentine would actually look like. She had been running on the assumption that she had to refrain from showing this unseen card because she didn't have it. How carefully would this drug dealer look to see if a card in Essie's walker basket was the actual card she had received or a substitute?

She quickly got busy. Her first thought was the sack full of greeting cards in the lower left-hand drawer of her desk. She pulled it out. There were some cards in her sack that she never used—mostly because they seemed inappropriate for any of her children or grandchildren. She now selected several of these and pondered them. One was long, thin, and black. Essie didn't know why she even kept it in her sack. She couldn't imagine giving anyone a black birthday card, even though the sentiment on the card was appropriate. Another card was a get well card. It was flowery, but the message was obviously one designed for a sick person. There were actually two valentines in the sack. Why she had never sent either of these was abundantly clear to Essie as she stared at them. Both were excessively gushy with ribbons and bows and little birds flying around the edges on one. As she tried to choose which one was the best choice for her purposes, she contemplated primarily the size, shape, and color of the envelopes. She realized that the crook would see the envelope first. Indeed, the crook might not even look inside when he was swiping the card from her basket.

She chose a valentine designed for one spouse to give another. It said "To my beloved" which was similar to the greeting on the front of the secret admirer card. Taking it with her and putting away the other cards, she brought the valentine to her desk and placed it on the blotter in the center. The first step was to sign the inside of the card, "your secret admirer" in a handwriting as similar as possible to that she remembered on the original. When that was completed, she turned to the front of the card. She realized that it would be important to convey at least a sense that this card had some thickness to it as did the original— thickness caused by the cocaine-filled heart in the center. She searched in her desk drawers looking for something that she could use to construct a heart. In a lower drawer, she found an old photograph album that had some pages comprised of gold leaf. *Hmm*, she thought. *It's not the pink like the original, but it does have the requisite fancy quality.* She pulled apart the pages and used her scissors to cut a large segment of the foil. Then, she fashioned a three-dimensional heart out of the material. Not perfect, but at a glance, the little gold heart would do in a pinch. She then realized she would need something to provide bulk to the heart's interior. She settled on a bunched up tissue that she glued inside the heart. Just before she glued the heart to the front of the card, however, she got another idea. She rolled over to her kitchen and rummaged through her drawers. Far in the back of one drawer, she grabbed a box of small sandwich bags, similar to those the police had used to collect the cocaine from her lap. She extracted one from the box and returned to her desk. Here, she searched through her desk drawers, eventually pulling out some small rubber bands, mending tape, glue, and a bottle of ink. Carefully, she filled one corner of the plastic bag with about a tablespoon of ink and then tightly bound the top with the tiny rubber band. Then she folded this little contraption inside the tissue paper, inside the gold foil heart on the front of the card, applying glue to the entire unit. She arranged it in such a way that anyone opening the envelope would find the heart tightly attached to the card. Any attempt to pull it off or detach it would result in the baggie breaking, and ink pouring out. At least, that was what she hoped would happen. She wasn't going to test it on herself because she didn't want black hands. She hoped this method would work. She hoped it would help her catch the drug dealer and keep herself safe in the process.

Before she put the card in the envelope, she turned the envelope over and considered how to make the front look as realistic as possible. Obviously, she couldn't supply a real postmark. She could, however, address it to herself and write in that phony return address that she clearly remembered from the original envelope.   Then she contemplated the upper right hand corner where she knew a stamp would go. She reached over in her middle desk drawer where she kept a supply of postage stamps. As she held the roll of stamps in her hands, she bit her lip and shook her head. No, this wouldn't work. An unused stamp just wouldn't look right. She put the stamps back in the drawer and reached to the top of her desk in the upper right hand corner where she kept a pile of important mail. She peeked into the pile and extracted an envelope that had a postage stamp on it which appeared fairly loose. Using her letter opener, she pushed and prodded the stamp until it finally gave way. With the used stamp in her hand, she placed a small dab of glue on its back and gently placed it in the upper right-hand corner of her fake envelope. Then, she grabbed a liner pen with black ink. It had a felt-tip and it worked well in labeling envelopes and other things. She practiced using some blank paper first. Looking at postmarks from some of her other envelopes, she drew postmarks with Boston, MA, and the previous day's date. She drew dozens of these marks, until she felt she was able to produce one that bore a reasonable facsimile to the one that had been on the original envelope. Then, as carefully as she was able, she drew the postmark across the old stamp on the fake envelope. When she had finished, she set down her pen and held the envelope up at a distance.

"Now, would I fall for this?" she asked herself. "Would I believe that this was an actual piece of mail that Essie Cobb received from a secret admirer?"

The answer to the question was a qualified 'yes.' There was nothing more she could do. Her trap was set. Now all she had to do was set it in motion. She carefully placed the fake envelope on the top of the pile of items in her walker basket and put down the lid. She pushed her walker into her bedroom and crawled under the covers. She always had her walker next to her bedside in case she needed to go to the bathroom but now there was another reason. She could keep her eye on it. If the Happy Haven drug dealer tried to take the card, he'd have to come in to get it, and maybe, just maybe, Essie might be awake and see him.

Chapter Twenty One

*"Love is an act of endless forgiveness, a tender look which
becomes a habit."*

—Peter Ustinov

Essie opened her eyes. Bright sunlight surrounded her. She
glanced over to her bedroom window and realized that it
was morning and that she had slept through the night. She
hadn't even needed a potty break. As she smiled in pride at
her bladder's achievement, the sudden realization of her
intended middle of the night goal surfaced. What about her
fake valentine? Had the drug dealer sneaked into her room
and snatched it? Essie stretched her legs out over the edge
of her bed and set her feet carefully in her bedroom slippers
on the floor. Bending over, she pulled her walker closer to
her and lifted the seat.

The cream-colored envelope sat untouched on top. Essie
picked it up and peeked inside. Her little heart remained
intact. Her trap was still unsprung. Essie didn't know
whether to be relieved or dismayed. If the person had
come in last night, she doubted she would have awakened
as she obviously had slept more soundly than usual. But
now she had to consider how to convey to the drug dealer
that his supply of cocaine was in her walker and just waiting
for him to come and retrieve it.

She sighed and lifted herself from her bed. Every bone and
joint creaked, but Essie had learned years ago to ignore
their noises. She realized that her body was somewhat like
a railroad train. It was slow to get moving, but once the

wheels started turning, it could go at an amazing speed. She gave each knee a little in-place bending until her lower extremities were functioning satisfactorily. Now upright, she grabbed her walker and headed into her bathroom. She couldn't remember the last time her bladder had maintained a full night's worth of liquid. *You go, little bladder*, she said to herself softly. Sometimes, she felt, body parts needed their own pep talks. Bladders, especially.

As she rolled back to her bed, DeeDee, her morning aide, knocked, called out her name, and then immediately showed up in her bedroom. Essie waited for DeeDee to bring her outfit that she had laid out the night before. Arthritis prevented Essie from dressing herself with any speed, so DeeDee made this morning ritual whiz by. In fact, she and DeeDee had such a well-practiced rhythm that Essie often thought they could enter a dressing contest if such a thing existed.

"Happy Valentine's Day, Miss Essie," DeeDee said as she pulled Essie's brown slacks on and up her thin legs. "The whole place is talking about this valentine you got from a secret admirer!"

Essie smiled. Her efforts were obviously working. She hadn't discussed the card with DeeDee and this was the first she'd heard her morning aide mention it. DeeDee loved gossip and she loved to tease Essie, especially about her love life, of which there wasn't any.

"It's true, DeeDee," replied Essie. "I got a lovely valentine from an admirer." She tried to blush coyly, but her acting skills were not what she wished they would be. She was much better at figuring out mysteries than pretending feelings she didn't have.

"That's romantic, Essie!" cried DeeDee, now working on tying Essie's tennis shoes. "Do you have any idea who sent it?"

"Not a clue," replied Essie. Of course, this was true, but DeeDee didn't need to know any more than that.

"I'd love to see it," said her aide, now standing and offering her arm to help Essie rise from her bed.

"I guess it's okay," said Essie hesitantly. She didn't want to let anyone inspect her makeshift card too closely or they would see how she had jerry-rigged it to include the trap. On the other hand, she did want to make sure that DeeDee saw enough that she remembered the card and would be sure to spread the story to all of her co-workers and other residents at Happy Haven. Essie bent down and lifted the lid of her walker.

"I see you take it with you," noted DeeDee as Essie brought out the cream-colored envelope.

"It's very precious to me," replied Essie. *Eeek*, she thought, *how corny. I wonder if DeeDee will fall for this folderol. She knows me so well. She knows that I'm not easily bamboozled. I can't believe she'd think for one minute that I'd become all mushy over a sentimental card from someone I didn't even know.* She clutched the envelope to her chest before reaching inside and carefully bringing out the frilly valentine.

"Oh, my!" exclaimed DeeDee, as she stared at the fake card that Essie held. "How beautiful!"

DeeDee's face looked awash with wonder. Essie bit her lip to keep from scoffing. Certainly she was proud of her own art work. When this was all over, she'd have to brag to Mindy about how she had created such a crafty card that fooled at least one person.

"It is, isn't it?" Essie beamed. She fluttered her eyelashes at DeeDee in her most girlish fashion.

"Could I see it?" asked DeeDee cautiously.

"Oh," replied Essie, clasping the card to her bosom in mock horror. "It just...means so much to me... DeeDee. I just hate to let it out of my sight. You understand, don't you?" She gave DeeDee her most soulful look and prayed that her friendly, daily aide wouldn't detect the playacting.

"Of course, sweetie!" answered DeeDee, patting Essie's shoulder warmly. "Believe me, if I ever got something so romantic, I'd guard it like Fort Knox too!" DeeDee chuckled under her breath and headed into Essie's bathroom where she typically cleaned up her sink and made sure Essie had enough toilet paper available each day.

Essie sighed in relief. It wasn't as hard to fool people as she thought it might be. She didn't know if she'd be able to handle things around Happy Haven in a similar fashion. She needed to make sure that everyone knew she had the card and that it was in her walker seat. But, she had to be very careful not to actually let anyone get a hold of it or they'd run the risk of spoiling her art work and the little trap she had set for the drug dealer.

"You think it's one of your beaux here at HH?" called out DeeDee from the bathroom. Essie rolled into the living room and pushed her walker over to her recliner. DeeDee eventually joined her and began to prepare Essie's morning pills.

"I don't have any beaux," said Essie curtly.

"Oh, I don't know about that!" shot back DeeDee, pouring water into her glass at Essie's sink. "That Hubert Darby follows you around like a puppy dog, Essie. You know that."

"Maybe," she replied. "But he's just one and he's not very aggressive."

"Aggressive!" said DeeDee, laughing. "You want your men to be more aggressive? Why, Essie I never would have guessed!"

"No," said Essie, shaking her head and scowling as she took her pills and water from DeeDee. "I mean I like that he's not aggressive. He's less bother that way."

"Bother!" said DeeDee with a twinkle. "Since when is having a male admirer a bother?"

"When you're ninety!" answered Essie. "I have enough to worry about without some fellow prancing around behind me like some sort of lovesick teenager."

"Lovesick teenager?" DeeDee asked. "Is that what Hubert does?"

"Him and that Dave Esperti," noted Essie, handing the glass back to DeeDee.

"Oh! Now, see, there are two of them!" said DeeDee, pointing at Essie in victory. "I knew you had more than one guy chasing after you. Since when has Dave been added to the list?"

"Not my list," replied Essie. "The only man on my list is my late husband John."

"I note your loyalty, Miss Essie," said DeeDee, squatting down beside her patient. "But surely your husband wouldn't begrudge you a little love in your... now that he's no longer here."

"He wouldn't," said Essie definitively, "but, DeeDee, I would begrudge it. John is the only man I ever loved and ever will love. That's all there is to it." Essie had not intended to get into such a personal discussion with her aide, but DeeDee was always a good listener and always so sympathetic. Essie had spoken many times to her about her late husband and DeeDee knew the special bond they'd shared.

"You're a wonderful lady, Miss Essie," said DeeDee, standing and giving Essie a brief hug. "If you ever do decide to give your heart away again, believe me, that will be some lucky man!" She headed over to the sink and replaced the glass. She straightened up Essie's small kitchen and then headed for the door.

"So, maybe this secret admirer is a possibility?" she asked. "I mean, if you don't think he's someone here at Happy Haven. Who could he be?"

"I don't know," replied Essie. "That's the romance of it, actually. If I knew who he was, then I'd have to deal with him. As long as I don't know, it remains a magical mystery."

"It certainly does," agreed DeeDee. She opened the door. "Hey, you'll have to ask that love guru! You know, the one who's speaking today!"

"Oh, DeeDee, I don't hold much stock in those types of individuals," said Essie, realizing that she hadn't actually used this morning's opportunity to pick DeeDee's brain regarding what her fellow workers knew about Essie's card. "I don't suppose that anyone has said anything about my secret admirer, have they?"

"Miss Essie," replied DeeDee, carefully closing the door but still holding it, "I told you, your secret admirer is the talk of the place!"

"Oh, you say that!" chided Essie, "but I can't believe people are actually interested in some greeting card I got."

"Oh, believe me, they are," replied DeeDee.

"What are they saying?" Essie asked.

"I don't know, just that you got a valentine from a secret admirer," said DeeDee. "The ladies are all jealous."

"You mean the residents," said Essie.

"And the staff," answered DeeDee. "Most women don't get flowery cards like that from their regular boyfriends or husbands, let alone someone they don't even know!"

"Are the men saying anything?" she prodded.

"Yeah," replied DeeDee, "some are. Mostly they're annoyed that your admirer makes all men look bad!" She laughed. "All men need to look bad once in a while. They should treat women better like your admirer does, Essie."

"Have you heard anything else?" Essie asked.

"I don't know what you mean," scowled DeeDee, furrowing her brow.

"I don't know," said Essie. "Just any questions or comments. I'm just curious, DeeDee." She smiled her fake smile again, hoping DeeDee wouldn't be put off by her probing.

"I believe I did hear someone say that one of the other residents had received a valentine from a secret admirer, but I don't remember who it was."

"Was it Betsy Rollingford?" asked Essie.

"I don't know her. It could be. I don't remember," replied DeeDee. "Do you want me to find out?"

"Oh, no!" said Essie quickly. The last thing she needed was to arouse suspicion by having DeeDee go on some fact-finding mission for her. That would be just the thing to call attention to herself and to her attempt to track down her secret admirer. *Yes, just the thing.* DeeDee waved good-bye and Essie was left alone to plan her next step.

Chapter Twenty Two

"All love that has not friendship for its base, is like a mansion built upon sand."

—Ella Wheeler Wilcox

Breakfast proved to be quite special. The chef had prepared a Valentine's Day treat for all the residents—heart-shaped pancakes covered with strawberries. A sprinkling of powdered sugar garnished the top. The whole dish was enchantingly pretty, thought Essie. It was a nice break from the usual fare.

"Happy Valentine's Day," Santos had greeted them. The juice was even themed for the day—pomegranate—a bright red. It was something Essie had never tasted before. She decided after a few sips that she preferred orange juice, but she was always willing to try something new.

"So, Essie," whispered Marjorie when the meals had all been delivered. "Anything new to report on... you know what?" Marjorie bent low and looked around suspiciously.

"There's no faulting your spy credentials, Marjorie," said Essie with a sneer. "Let's try not to call attention to ourselves. All right?"

"No one is doing that, Essie," replied Opal, in defense of Marjorie. "You can't expect us not to be curious about what's going on after...everything that occurred yesterday." She covered her mouth discreetly with her napkin when she said this last part.

"No one is looking at us or paying us the least attention," replied Essie as she glanced around the dining hall. Indeed, all the residents seemed far more interested in their festive pancakes than they were in overhearing the conversations at any nearby tables.

"I hope someone is paying attention to us," said Opal. "I mean Detective Abbott did say they'd have an undercover agent keeping an eye out for our drug dealer." Opal again patted her mouth as she mumbled this sentence.

"If there is someone watching us, they're certainly being very discreet," noted Essie. Then, almost to herself she added, "Maybe that's why no one came into my room last night."

"What?" asked Marjorie, her head inclined towards Essie politely. "Essie, you said you were going to personally track down the...individual in question...and you weren't going to let the warnings from the... authorities...stand in your way."

"And I still believe that, Marjorie," said Essie. "But I'm going about it with delicacy and not like a bull in a china shop."

"Is that how you think I would do it?" asked Marjorie, slapping her napkin in her lap.

"No, of course not," replied Essie calmly. "I just want you all to know that I did take the warnings we received yesterday to heart, and although I don't intend to follow those warnings to the letter, I do intend to honor their spirit."

"Now, what does that mean, Essie?" asked Opal skeptically. She adjusted her eyeglasses and peered over the edges at her friend.

"Yes, Essie," added Marjorie, "just what is it you intend to do?"

"What I already have done!" said Essie sweetly. She reached over to her walker and opened the seat. From inside she pulled out the cream-colored envelope that contained the fake card. She held it up in front of her chest so her tablemates could see it.

"What is that?" asked Opal.

"You know what it is," answered Essie in a low voice that contradicted her smiling face.

"I thought you... gave it to...you know," said Marjorie in a whisper, glancing around cautiously to see if any of the residents at the other tables had noticed the envelope that Essie was now displaying. No one seemed to be paying any attention to what was happening at Essie's table.

"Did the...authorities...uh, bring it back to you?" asked Opal, obviously confused, as she too looked around cautiously.

"No," said Essie calmly. "They still have it." She closed her mouth and looked wide-eyed at her friends. Even Fay stared at the envelope in apparent mystery.

"So, what is that?" asked Marjorie, nodding at the card.

"This is the card from my secret admirer," replied Essie, doing nothing to dispel the confusion.

"The one sent to you from Boston," added Opal.

"Not exactly," said Essie, with a slight shrug.

"You mean you received another card from your secret admirer?" asked Marjorie with excitement.

"No," said Essie. Then with a quick look around to be certain no one was listening, she whispered very softly, "I made it." She carefully opened the envelope and gently removed the card inside.

"What?" cried Marjorie.

"You heard me, Marjorie," said Essie. Still whispering, she continued, "I worked on it all last night. I gathered all of the material from old cards and things I had in my desk. I remembered what the original card looked like, so I made a duplicate out of those things. I tried my best to make it look like the one I got from the secret admirer. What do you think?" She held the card up a bit higher, almost to nose height and looked from one woman to another.

"It's amazing, actually," said Opal. It never occurred to me that it was a different card. The envelope is virtually identical, so I just assumed it was the same. I didn't really pay that much attention to the card itself, but when you showed it, it seemed like the other one. What do you think, Marjorie?"

"Me too!" agreed the brunette, eyes agog. "I can't believe you made that, Essie." She was having difficulty keeping her voice low with the obvious excitement she was experiencing. "Let me see it!" She reached over in an attempt to grab it from Essie. Essie quickly pulled it back.

"No!" she cried in a soft voice. "I can't let you do that."

"Why not?" asked Opal. "We're not going to tell anyone. We're on your side. Maybe if we look at it, we can give you some suggestions to improve it."

"I'm sure you could," said Essie, "but that's not the reason I can't let you see it. I can't really have anyone touching the little heart I made. It's rather delicate and it might fall apart and I'm just not sure I could put it back together again if it did. It took forever to get it the way it is now. You understand, don't you?" She gave her sickeningly sweet false smile, hoping against hope that her friends would go along with her and not demand to see—or worse yet, touch—the card itself.

"I'd be careful," whined Marjorie.

"Oh, I don't know, Marjorie," added Opal. "If she really doesn't want us to touch it. Can't you just hold it a little closer to us?"

"Opal," said Essie, pleading, "I really want to keep it under wraps. Of course, I want people here at Happy Haven to know I have it so they'll spread the word, but I don't want anyone to get a close view because they might mention a feature that isn't the same as the original and if the original sender got wind of that, he might be scared off."

"Oh, okay, Essie," said Marjorie. "I won't press you on it. Truly, I think this is a far-fetched and possibly dangerous idea, but I'll support you. And if you don't want me to see it any closer, so be it."

"Opal?"

"All right, Essie," replied Opal. She brought her palms together in prayer position, almost as if she were giving Essie her blessing.

"Fay?" asked Essie. Fay looked from Opal to Marjorie and then back to Essie. Finally, she nodded several times in agreement. Essie held the card to her chest and then out in front of her as she looked at it.

"More coffee, ladies?" asked Santos, appearing at Essie's side with a silver urn. Essie had no time to put the card back in its envelope. "Oh, Miss Essie! Is that card from your secret admirer?" Essie mumbled something and attempted to cover the card with the envelope.

"Um, Santos," said Opal, motioning him with her finger. "I'd like more coffee, please."

"Me too, Santos," added Marjorie. Fay pointed to her empty cup also. Their distractions allowed Essie time to slip the fake card back in its envelope. Santos quickly refilled all four cups.

"Did you find out who is secret admirer, Miss Essie?" he continued to probe, apparently unaware that Essie and her entire table were unwilling to discuss the matter.

"No," she replied, "actually, it's more romantic not to know, Santos! It would probably spoil it if I knew who it was!" By now, she had replaced the card in its envelope and put the envelope back in the basket beneath her walker seat.

"I believe there are many secret admirers for you here at Happy Haven, Miss Essie," continued Santos. "They secret only if you want them to be, Miss Essie. If you give these men a sign, Miss Essie, I am sure they will no longer be *secret* admirers." He smiled sweetly at her. Essie had assisted Santos with various endeavors in the past and she knew he appreciated her greatly—probably more than did many or most other people at Happy Haven.

"Well, that's not going to happen, Santos," replied Essie. "This secret admirer is going to stay that way—secret!"

"I not send card, Miss Essie," he said, now standing and holding the coffee pot with both hands, "but I am one of your admirers!" He smiled, and then suddenly recognized the implications of his statement. "Oh, not romantic, Miss Essie..."

"I should hope not!" Essie snorted.

"But I admire you like I admire my... madre!"

The other ladies at the table tittered at this unsolicited expression of devotion from the young waiter.

"If you admire me so much, Santos," said Essie, "then maybe you could help me out with a little question I have."

"Of course, Miss Essie," he replied, jiggling up and down a bit in anticipation of Essie's request.

"Could you tell me why you're delivering meals to Grace Bloom?" she asked. Santos's smile disappeared. He quickly looked from Essie to her friends and back.

"Miss Essie," he said, shaking his head. "I don't know what you're talking about! I not deliver meals to Miss Bloom. Need to get back to kitchen now. Hope you find secret admirer. Good-bye, Miss Essie. Ladies." He gave a quick bow and then virtually sprinted back into the kitchen.

"Essie," cried Opal, "that was horrible! You put that poor young man on the spot!"

"I put *him* on the spot?" retorted Essie.

"Yes," replied Opal. "He obviously didn't want to tell you about Grace Bloom, or maybe he couldn't tell you about Grace Bloom."

"Why not?" Essie asked. "What's so secret about a resident getting meals in her room? If she's ill, I'd like to know so I can visit her or do something nice for her."

"You think Grace is ill?" asked Marjorie.

"Of course not," said Essie. "I saw her in line for dinner last night. And the other day I actually knocked on her door and she answered. She didn't seem at all sick to me. Although, she wouldn't let me in her room or even see inside her room."

"That doesn't surprise me, Essie," noted Opal. "You can be a bit pushy. Grace doesn't know you like we do."

"Thanks for the vote of confidence, Opal," Essie said with a huff. "But mark my word; there is something fishy going on there."

"Well, you don't have time to worry about Grace Bloom and track down your secret admirer too," explained Opal. "You'd better focus on one or the other."

"Don't be ridiculous, Opal," said Essie. "Haven't you heard of multi-tasking?"

"I'd focus on the letter if I were you," suggested Marjorie. "It has the potential for being much more dangerous."

"You don't know that, Marjorie," said Essie.

"You think Grace Bloom presents some sort of threat to us?" asked Marjorie.

"No," replied Essie, "but something strange is going on in her room and I intend to find out. Just like I intend to find my...secret admirer." She eyed her walker basket knowingly.

"Just be careful, Essie," said Opal, shaking her finger in Essie's direction.

"Yes, Essie, be careful," added Marjorie, also extending a finger of admonition. As two fingers came at her from both sides of the table, Essie looked up at silent Fay in her wheelchair. The chubby little woman looked around at her friends and then extended her index finger directly at Essie.

Chapter Twenty Three

"Love is an irresistible desire to be irresistibly desired."

—Robert Frost

Leaving the dining hall, Essie stopped briefly at her mail box to see if the morning mail had arrived. It had. In fact, included among all the regular junk mail, there were two envelopes with her name hand written on the front. Just her name—no address. The cards had just been dropped in the Happy Haven mail for Phyllis to distribute. *Oh, no!* she thought. *Someone—obviously someone here at Happy Haven—had probably sent her valentines. And she hadn't purchased valentines for anyone. It couldn't be Marjorie or Fay or Opal. The four of them had agreed long ago not to indulge in such wasteful practices. They merely wished each other verbal greetings on various holidays.* Essie piled her mail in her basket on top of her fake valentine and headed off towards her apartment.

When she reached her room, she plopped down in her recliner and drew out the pile of mail. *First things first,* she thought. She opened one of the greeting cards. It was definitely a valentine. Not as flowery or profuse as the one from her secret admirer, but a very nice card just the same. She opened the card and read the message inside. It was simple but sweet. The card was signed, "With all my heart, Hubert." *That is nice,* she thought. Hubert had a great deal of trouble expressing his feelings orally, so sending her a card was a natural approach for the exceedingly shy man. Over the years, Essie had tried to bolster Hubert's confidence and be a good friend to him. She knew that Hubert longed for a more emotional arrangement, but that would never be possible and Essie did everything she could to dissuade him without thoroughly destroying his delicate ego.

She set Hubert's card aside and picked up the second envelope. She opened it and also found a sweet valentine. This one featured little bears in human clothes expressing very human sentiments. It was charming and certainly not too cloying. The message inside made her chuckle. It was signed "Dave Esperti." *Hmmm,* she thought, *I didn't think Dave could be this considerate. I just thought he was an inveterate flirt. I wonder if he sent cards like this to all the women at Happy Haven. I wouldn't put it past him.* She laughed. It was a relief that the two valentines were from actual people she knew and not from some unknown secret admirer. If that were the case, she would simply pull out her hair.

"Residents!" sang out Phyllis's voice over the Intercom. "Don't forget our big event this afternoon! Dr. Love, otherwise known as the Guru of Romance will be speaking in the lobby at two o'clock. He'll tell us all about the history of romantic love AND he'll answer your questions about love and romance. Now isn't that a perfect program for Valentine's Day!" Phyllis gushed some more as she provided the background of the speaker who was actually an anthropology professor from the local college—Grace University. Essie was sure that most residents would probably attend because it sounded like it would be FUN (according to Phyllis), and most of the residents always enjoyed FUN programs. Essie, however, considered such events a waste of time. She would much rather be doing something constructive. And right now, the most constructive thing she could think of doing was finding out who the secret admirer, alias Happy Haven drug dealer, was. She had waved the fake card around at breakfast, but decided that she needed to flaunt it a bit more if she was going to be sure that the unknown dealer was aware that she still had it.

She made a much needed bathroom trip and then returned to her recliner where she whipped off several puzzles she had been working on. *Nothing like a good puzzle to tweak the little brain cells,* she told herself. She knew she had to be in top mental and physical form (as top as that form could be for a ninety-year-old lady) when she battled wits with the Happy Haven drug dealer. She'd have to think of a better name for him. As she didn't know who it was, it didn't seem right to constantly refer to him as *a him*. It might be a woman. In fact, it most likely was a woman as women outnumbered men at Happy Haven eight to one—at least among the residents. She surmised that the proportion was probably somewhat similar among the staff too. Most of the nurses' aides were women, although she tended to think that the kitchen staff was more equally divided between men and women. As for the upper management, now that she thought about It, they were all female. Indeed, the Happy Haven drug dealer most likely was a woman. *How disgusting*, she thought. She couldn't even imagine a woman doing something as vile as selling drugs—particularly a woman who worked at an assisted living facility. She knew that everyone who worked at Happy Haven was not a saint but she wanted to believe that the staff there was one of the kindest and most thoughtful anywhere. How was it possible that someone who she may have considered a sweet, gentle person for years had actually been making a profit selling illegal drugs?

She gave up this useless line of reasoning and headed out into the family room. Amazingly enough, Dave and Hubert were playing cards with Betsy and Nadine again. They obviously were a happy foursome. *It was a perfect set-up,* thought Essie. *They can keep playing and I'll just plant a little bit of information among the four.* She rolled over slowly, smiling at other residents who were seated in the family room.

"I played that card, Hubert!" shouted Dave at his partner. The two women smiled and attempted to contain their delight. Hubert slammed his cards on the table.

"I don't like to play with you," Hubert pouted.

"Now, Hubert," said Betsy softly, patting Hubert's hand. "It was an easy mistake. It happens to me all the time." She smiled sweetly at him and he blushed and looked down.

"Really, Dave," scolded Nadine. "It's just a game."

Essie pushed her walker to the corner of the table, right between Hubert and Betsy.

"Hello," she said. "This sounds like a very exciting game!"

"It is when you have a partner who knows what he's doing!" shouted Dave to Hubert. Hubert pulled his head down into his big body like a giant ostrich.

"Actually," Essie continued, "I wanted to stop by and thank you for the lovely valentine."

"Oh, you're welcome, Essie," replied Dave. His eyes suddenly changed from anger at Hubert to flirtatious merriment. "Hope it makes you forget that silly petticoat-looking one you got from that loony secret admirer. I send cards to all my girls." He smiled in a smarmy way at the other women at the table and they both beamed back at him.

"Did you get my card, Miss Essie?" Hubert asked, raising his head maybe an inch from his shoulders.

"Yes, Hubert, I did," said Essie. "I loved it!" Hubert glowed. Dave sneered and began to shuffle the cards for the next round.

"Do you want to join our game, Miss Essie?" Hubert asked.

"Oh, thank you for asking, Hubert," she replied, "but I really just stopped by to thank you both for the valentines. My goodness! I don't know when I've received so many lovely cards." She reached down into her basket and pulled the fake valentine from her basket. "It's amazing how beautiful some valentines are, isn't it?" She carefully slipped the fake card from the envelope and held it up adoringly. "Isn't this card beautiful? This is the one my secret admirer sent!"

Dave snorted and focused on his cards. Hubert looked forlorn. Betsy gave Essie a confused look followed by a subtle warning glance. Only Nadine responded in the way Essie hoped. She gushed.

"Oh, Essie!" Nadine cried. "That's gorgeous! Do you have any idea who your admirer is?"

"No," said Essie. "All I know is that it was postmarked Boston. I've thought and thought about anyone I might know or have known in Boston, but I just can't think of anyone. Of course, it could be someone I met somewhere else who moved to Boston. You know, Nadine, I've lived here in Reardon all my life. Anyone who knew me many years ago might be able to guess that I still lived here and be able to track me down. It's not as if Reardon is that large or that there are that many Essie Cobbs who live here."

"That's true! He could remember you even if you don't remember him!" said Nadine in a romantic fog.

Several staff members walked by without paying attention to the group at the table. Essie waved the card around, attempting to make sure that the two staffers saw the valentine.

"Maybe he'll get in touch with you!" Nadine suggested. "I mean, maybe sending you this valentine is just the beginning. He might want to rekindle a romance from long ago."

"I can't think of anyone I had any romances with long ago," said Essie, genuinely contemplating her past loves, and then suddenly remembering that the secret admirer did not actually know her, but was just using her mailbox as a drop off for his illegal drugs. *How easy it is to get wrapped up in these stories*, she thought.

"I don't know why you'd want some unknown guy in Boston," said Dave, jumping into the conversation, "when you have two perfectly fine men here at Happy Haven." He looked over at Hubert, with a sort of apologetic smile.

"Yeah," agreed Hubert, protruding his lower lip and nodding in agreement. "Two perfectly fine men right here." This last sentence was obviously much too aggressive for him and his face turned a beet red and he hid it in his shirt collar.

"You're right," said Essie to the men at the table. "If this secret admirer really cared for me, he wouldn't remain hidden. He'd sign his card like a gentleman. Like the two of you did!" She nodded sharply to drive home her point. The men seemed satisfied. "Even so," she added, "I can't help but be curious. I mean, you all would be curious if you got a card like this from someone who signed it 'secret admirer' wouldn't you?"

"I know I would!" cried Nadine.

"I'd probably forget all about it," said Betsy with another veiled warning.

"Who'd send me a card like that?" asked Hubert. The poor man sounded so pitiful, Essie couldn't help but feel her heart break for him.

"I guess I'd be just like you, Essie," said Dave finally. "That's how we're alike. We're both spitfires and we don't just let things alone. When we see a way to fix things or change something, we do it!"

Boy oh joy! Essie thought. She hoped that she wasn't just like Dave Esperti. True, he was headstrong and outspoken, somewhat like her. But that was where the similarities ended, she hoped.

"I guess I'd better get going," said Essie, satisfied that she had displayed the secret admirer valentine sufficiently for numerous passersby to see it. She slipped it back in her basket and headed over to the elevator.

"Hey, Essie!" Dave called after her. "Why don't you bring your secret admirer valentine to that Dr. Love this afternoon? I bet he'd be able to tell you who sent it to you!"

Essie ignored Dave's suggestion and waved at the group as the elevator door closed.

Chapter Twenty Four

"Never pretend to a love which you do not actually feel, for love is not ours to command."

—Alan Watts

On the second floor, Essie headed back to the rec room where the arts and crafts class was spending their last session making valentines. Sue Barber was again in the center of the tables describing final special touches that residents could add to their cards. Essie glanced over to the table where she had sat the previous day and noted that Donna, Velma, and their quiet friend were again hard at work on card construction. Apparently, Donna had finished her previous valentine, sent it to her deceased husband, and was now hard at work on a new work of art. Essie rolled over and slid comfortably into the empty seat.

"Essie!" said Velma from across the table. "Welcome back! Did your new great grandson like his valentine?"

"What?" said Essie, befuddled.

"The card you made yesterday," replied Velma, "for your new little great grandson. Remember?"

"Oh, yes!" said Essie, suddenly recalling her small fib. Now why had she made up such a ridiculous lie? She was trying to keep from hurting Donna's feelings by not mentioning her own husband, and here she just succeeded in creating a story that she'd now have to maintain for no reason.

"Oh, fine," she lied. "I'm going to work on another one now."

"For your great grandson?" asked Donna.

"Maybe," said Essie, vaguely. "What about you? Did you finish the card you were making yesterday? This one looks different."

"No," replied Donna, "it's the same one. I've just changed some things on it."

Some things, thought Essie. *The whole thing was more like it. Oh, well, to each her own. And it doesn't matter anyway if she's just going to give it to someone who's no longer here.*

Sue Barber was rambling on about it being Valentine's Day so it was their last chance to finish up the cards they were working on. Tomorrow, she said, they would be starting a new project. She demonstrated a way to trim card edges with gold filigree.

"I want some of that," said Velma when she saw the shiny thread sparkling from Sue's hands. "It would look really nice on my card. Don't you think, Essie?"

"Very nice," agreed Essie. She pushed around some paper in the center of the table as she pretended to show some interest in making another card.

"What about that card from your secret admirer?" asked Velma. "Did you ever find out who sent it?"

"No," replied Essie. *Now, we're getting somewhere*, she thought. *And here's a good test. The women at this table all actually saw the original card the other day. I wonder if they'll recognize that I've substituted a fake card or will they fall for my ploy?* She reached over to her walker basket and brought out the cream-colored envelope that contained the fake card. She held it to her chest in pretend adoration.

"It must really make you curious," said Donna. "Not knowing who this man is who sent you this beautiful card."

"It does," said Essie, providing her table companions with a deep, romantic sigh. "Here he is longing for me but not having the courage to reveal himself. I may never find out who he is."

"That's horrible to think," said Donna, "but still very romantic. You and he are like unrequited lovers!" She clasped her arms to her chest and sighed deeply too. The other two women smiled and appeared to repeat the same heartfelt sigh.

"I guess we are," agreed Essie, taking the envelope and peeking inside at the card. She pulled it slightly out of the envelope as she stared longingly at the front. She was careful not to let the little fake heart she had created move past the edge of the envelope flap. She wanted to make certain that the women still believed that she possessed the card without actually allowing them to get a close view of it.

Sue Barber was now moving around the room as she had done the other day, commenting on each resident's homemade cards.

"Oh, my, Donna!" she declared as she reached Essie's table. "You've totally redone your card!" *Redone!* thought Essie. *Sue Barber was obviously more observant than she was. To her eye, Donna's card looked totally different too.*

"Essie," said Sue, "I see you're still pondering your secret admirer card."

"Yes, Miss Barber," replied Essie. "I thought about all the things you told me yesterday. You really got me thinking about this card. I still don't know who sent it, but I intend to find out. I do!"

"Good for you!" replied Sue, barely glancing at the fragment of card sticking out of the envelope. "Are you going to make another card? Maybe one you can send to that admirer when you discover his identity?" She smiled at Essie and Essie realized that the sub-text was that this was arts and crafts class and if Essie was going to be here she should actually be doing arts and crafts.

"Oh, yes, Miss Barber!" exclaimed Essie. "I'm just trying to figure out what colors to use!" She quickly grabbed a few sheets of craft paper and a pair of scissors and began snipping away.

"Wonderful!" said Sue. "I can't wait to see what you create!" She moved on to the next table and the women returned to their gluing and cutting.

Smooth, Essie thought. *Apparently, Sue Barber believes my fake valentine is the original. She didn't appear the least bit suspicious. Neither do any of the women at this table and they all saw the real card.*

"My goodness, Essie," whispered Velma, "you're clutching that valentine like it's your long lost child! No one's going to take it from you."

Essie jolted from her reverie. Velma's words struck her because, indeed, she did expect someone to take it from her.

"Oh, you know!" said Essie, with a casual laugh, "it's not every day that a girl gets a card from a secret admirer." She gave the women a coy look.

"Yes," agreed Donna, "it's very nice." With that, she returned to her cutting and pasting as did the others. All the excitement the women had shown the other day over her card appeared to have vanished.

"Weren't those delicious pancakes this morning?" Velma asked the entire group. Everyone nodded their assent, including the silent lady to Essie's left. "The strawberries were so sweet. And that pomegranate juice!"

"I love how the chef created such a nice theme for Valentine's Day!" added Donna.

"I wonder what he'll do for lunch and dinner," said Velma. At that, the other ladies had an entirely new topic of interest. They all mused over possible menu items for Valentine's Day for the next several minutes.

"Oh, are you all going to that special presentation by that Dr. Love?" asked Velma enthusiastically. "That sounds like a lot of fun. They have him billed as the 'guru of love'! He is supposed to answer questions from the audience about love and romance!"

"I'm going to ask him about my husband," said Donna.

"Donna," said Velma, in what Essie considered an unnecessarily harsh voice, "your husband is dead."

"I'm going to ask him about my husband," Donna repeated as if she hadn't even heard Velma's comment.

"Essie," declared Velma, turning to the newest member of the table, "you should ask the 'guru of love' about your secret admirer. I bet he can help you figure out who he is."

"I doubt it," replied Essie.

"You never know," added Donna. Essie glanced at the silent woman to her left who nodded knowingly.

"Well, I'll see," she said.

"Do any of you know Grace Bloom?" asked Essie suddenly.

"She plays Quiz Bowl," responded Velma. "A very nice lady. Her husband died too, Donna." Velma glanced over at Donna. "However, she knows he's gone."

"I know Grace," added Donna. "She's in my knitting club. Although she hasn't come lately."

"I told you, Donna," chided Velma, "her husband died recently. Maybe she's having trouble adjusting—like you."

"I'm not having any trouble adjusting," said Donna calmly. "My husband isn't dead."

"Oh, why bother?" cried Velma, flinging her hands in the air.

"Grace's husband lived here at Happy Haven with her?" asked Essie.

"I believe so," replied Velma, with an annoyed glance towards Donna. "I believe they moved here when he retired. He was a vet."

"In the military?" asked Essie.

"No," said Velma, "an animal doctor. Grace was his nurse. They had a clinic in Reardon for many years."

"That's nice," said Essie. "I had heard that she was ill."

"Ill?" asked Velma. "I don't think so. I saw her at dinner the other night. Although, now that you mention it, she hasn't been at Quiz Bowl in quite some time. She used to be a regular."

"You saw her eating at dinner?" asked Essie.

"I think so," said Velma. "Donna, didn't you see Grace Bloom at dinner the other night?"

"Yes," said Donna. "She was there. I'm sure of it." Essie wondered how sure Donna was of Grace Bloom's attendance at dinner when she wasn't sure of her own husband's existence. Oh, well, Essie realized that sometimes elderly people had blind spots about certain issues and were still quite astute on everything else. Possibly Donna did understand everything except her husband's death. Even so, she thought, Velma's rather harsh behavior towards her friend's problem seemed unnecessarily cruel.

As Essie looked around the table, it was clear that the other women had completed beautiful homemade valentines. Essie had completed nothing. She sat as she had day before, a glue bottle in her hand, squeezing white goop around the edges of a big red construction paper heart. She knew her art work was not well done, but then she also knew that the art work she had done last night that now resided inside the envelope in her walker basket was truly a work of art. It didn't really matter how well this present project fared. She smiled sheepishly at the other women who all looked at her handiwork pitifully.

"Guess I'm just not much of an artist," Essie said to the women.

"Don't worry, Essie," said Donna sweetly. "So you're not an artist! You have other talents!"

"Yes," agreed Velma. "Everyone at Happy Haven knows about your talents, Essie. You're our resident detective."

Essie smiled. Little did Velma know how true it was. For indeed, Essie was deep in the throes of ferreting out her secret admirer who was also the local drug dealer. She believed she had sufficiently flaunted her envelope around in the arts and crafts class. She was quite certain that the three women at this table and Sue Barber, who all had actually seen the card yesterday, had been fooled by her ruse. Now, whether or not they would convey that information to other people—other people who would hopefully include the suspect of interest—was uncertain. But she had taken the first step.

It was getting late, and Sue Barber was instructing the arts and crafts class to finish up their cards and put their supplies away. Essie assisted her tablemates in taking items back to cupboards on the side walls. Eventually, when the room was picked up, she bid farewell to her three new friends and headed out of the rec room. As she rolled down the second floor hallway towards the elevator she contemplated where she might go next to cautiously seed her story and show various Happy Haven residents and staff members peeks of the card itself. The elevator door opened and Essie entered.

Chapter Twenty Five

"Love is a canvas furnished by Nature and embroidered by imagination."

—Voltaire

As she exited the elevator on the first floor, the family room was almost deserted. Probably most of the residents were in their rooms, getting ready for lunch. The lobby looked fairly empty too. Only Phyllis was visible, standing guard of the front desk as she usually did. Essie rolled casually over and began to peruse the array of sign-up sheets all lined up on the counter with their pencils attached with strings.

"Library field trip tomorrow, Essie!" Phyllis warbled, and pointed out a purple sheet that contained at least a dozen signatures.

"Oh, not this week, Phyllis," replied Essie politely. "I've got enough reading material in my room." This wasn't actually true, but Essie hated field trips. She hated being more than a quick roll from the nearest bathroom and she wasn't going to be forced to wear those disgusting adult diapers. She continued to look at the clipboards of sheets on the counter.

"You surely won't miss Dr. Love this afternoon, will you?" the desk clerk asked Essie breathlessly. *You'd think it was Clark Gable making an appearance today rather than some academic with a made-up nickname.* She doubted that Dr. Love really knew anything about love—or at least any more about love than the average person.

"I don't know," she said sweetly. "I'll have to see what's on my schedule."

"You could show the Doctor that valentine you got!" suggested Phyllis suddenly.

"Oh, I wouldn't feel comfortable doing that," replied Essie. "It's rather personal and I really don't want to tell everyone about it." *Ooops*, she thought.

"Really?" asked Phyllis skeptically. "I thought I saw you showing that card around all over the place."

"Just to a few friends," said Essie, cringing. "Phyllis, that does remind me, I wanted to ask you about the mail."

"You mean more than you asked the other day?" asked the clerk, tipping her head incredulously.

"Yes, actually," said Essie. "I'm just curious. You know, all this valentine talk has got me to thinking about the mail and how we get our mail. We do get mail every day and you are the person responsible for delivering it!" Essie felt she was buttering up Phyllis properly.

"It's not always me," noted Phyllis. "Sometimes one of the other staff members distributes it when I'm busy doing something else."

"Oh?" asked Essie. "How often does that happen?"

"I don't know," replied Phyllis. "I don't keep a record. Most of the staff are willing to jump in and help when one of us gets behind." She smiled cordially at Essie as if to say *that should answer your question.*

"I'm just curious, Phyllis, about that little hallway behind the mailboxes," said Essie. "I can see you moving around back there sometimes when you're putting our mail in our boxes, and sometimes I even see other people back there. Is it some open area for the staff?"

"Actually," replied Phyllis, "it's a small hallway that runs around the back of the facility, from the back entrance to the kitchen. There are several entrance spots. We also use it for storage. You wouldn't believe all the boxes that are back there!" She laughed and then realized that Essie was not as caught up in this behind the scene look at Happy Haven as she was.

"So all staff members have access to that hallway?" asked Essie.

"Of course," replied Phyllis. "Most of us use it as a short-cut to the parking lot too."

"Hmm," noted Essie. "So, any staff member going through this back hallway could feasibly stop at the residents' mailboxes and remove their mail."

"Oh, no, Essie!" exclaimed Phyllis. "No one would do such a thing! Besides, the mailboxes can only be opened from behind with the mail master key—and I keep that at the front desk." She nodded succinctly as if to say that that should calm all of Essie's concerns.

"Who has access to that key?" Essie asked.

"Now, Essie," said Phyllis, "I can't understand why you're so concerned about the safety of your mail. Are you missing a letter you were expecting?" She eyed Essie with dismay.

"Oh, no!" said Essie, laughing lightly. "Nothing like that! Just curious, Phyllis. You know me, I'm curious about everything!"

"I do know you, Essie, and you are the curious one for sure! It's probably all this excitement over that secret admirer of yours. Maybe you think he's sent you another card and we've somehow failed to get it in your mailbox?" She tipped her head to the side, as if anticipating Essie's response.

"No, nothing like that," said Essie. "I have every faith that you deliver my mail correctly every single day, Phyllis. It's probably true, though, that getting that valentine from my secret admirer has made me much more interested in the mail these days."

"Well, that's understandable," said Phyllis. "I hear you carry that card with you everywhere!"

Hmm, thought Essie. *You've heard that, have you? That's good. It means my plan is working.* Essie reached down and opened her seat lid. She pulled out the envelope and held it up so Phyllis could see it.

"I do carry it with me," Essie said. She clutched the envelope with both hands and gave Phyllis a sickeningly sweet facial expression.

"Oh, Essie, dear," Phyllis sighed. "You don't need to worry. I know residents get worried about their mail. We once had a man who thought we had lost his Social Security check. We hadn't, of course. It was simply a day or two late in arriving, but the poor man was inconsolable. He contacted the government and was about ready to set forth a major investigation. We're really very careful about your mail. I promise."

Essie nodded as if she was a child and Phyllis was her mother giving her a lecture. All the while, she was contemplating the maze of hallways behind the mailboxes and the various people who had access to them. She looked around the front desk as Phyllis continued to ramble on about how careful Happy Haven was with residents' mail. On a small bulletin board on the wall behind the desk, a variety of keys hung from hooks. Each key had a marking on it. Essie guessed that the master key to the mailboxes that Phyllis had mentioned was hanging on this board—right out in public for anyone to grab, assuming they knew which key it was. And probably many staff members knew which key it was.

Phyllis continued to drone on and Essie continued to smile at her. As far as she could tell, almost any staff member would be able to extract mail from a resident's mailbox, or possibly grab a particular envelope before it even got placed in the resident's box. She started to think about things in reverse order, from the point of view of the dealer at Happy Haven. Whoever the person was must have some method for indicating to the Boston dealer who to send a particular cocaine-filled envelope to. It was likely that the Happy Haven dealer chose a resident at random and sent that resident's name and address to the Boston dealer who then sent the appropriate amount of cocaine to the Happy Haven dealer, via the mailbox of the indicated resident. The Happy Haven dealer would then be on the lookout for a certain type of envelope arriving for that particular resident that he or she had already indicated to the Boston dealer. Obviously, the Happy Haven dealer was not going to use the same resident over and over again for the drop, because if an envelope happened to slip through—as it had in Essie's case when Phyllis put it directly into her hands—the Happy Haven dealer would not want to use that resident again. Essie reasoned that a similar situation had probably happened with Betsy last year. Somehow, the cocaine-filled envelope slipped through the Happy Haven dealer's routine and got in Betsy's hands before the dealer could grab it. However, in Betsy's case, the dealer just waited until Betsy put the pretty valentine on her television set, slipped into Betsy's room when she was out, and grabbed it, with Betsy being none the wiser.

Busting britches! thought Essie suddenly. *There are obviously more envelopes with cocaine arriving at Happy Haven than just these two. The one I found and the one Betsy got are probably just the tip of the iceberg. Who knows how many little packets of cocaine are arriving here daily in the U.S. mail! The police know this. Supposedly, they have someone undercover keeping an eye on things.* She wondered if the undercover cop was looking for the drug dealer or was watching her to protect her. *Oh, well!* She couldn't spend her time worried about that.

Another thought crossed Essie's mind. *Why just valentines? Yes, her drug-filled card was a valentine and Betsy's card was a valentine. But that didn't mean that this drug scheme was restricted just to valentines. Why would a drug dealer function only during February? There were probably drugs arriving in birthday cards, anniversary cards, get well cards,*

Christmas cards, and every other kind of card anyone could imagine.

She wondered how long this scheme had been going on. *It was obviously a small enough plot that it simply didn't draw much attention to itself. It could have been going on for years. Who would suspect an old person who lived in an assisted living facility as being a drug dealer?*

Phyllis had wound down. She was patting Essie's hand. Hand patting always seemed to mean that the younger person who was speaking wanted to have the older person who was listening to them agree to what was being said and go about their business. Essie got the message. She thanked Phyllis and headed back to her room.

She by-passed her chair and went straight to her bed and plopped down on her spread. In a second, she was sound asleep.

When she awoke from her brief nap several minutes later, she was refreshed and hungry. *First things first.* She checked her walker basket. The card was still there, still in its envelope on the top of the pile. She didn't think anyone would come in during the day when they knew she was in her room, but one never knew. She rolled into her bathroom and did some quick ablutions in preparation for lunch.

Essie Cobb, you rascal! she said to her image in the mirror. *You managed to pull off this ridiculous ploy. You also managed to convince everyone that you are gaga over this unknown man. You'd think people around here knew you better than to believe that you'd be all doe-eyed over some fellow you've never met.* She grabbed her brush and fluffed up her beautiful, shiny white curls. Yes, she looked ninety, but she did have sparkling blue eyes and a killer smile. No wonder some guy in Boston had a crush on her—even if he was a fake.

I wonder if I've spread the word enough, she thought. *I can't be sure that the dealer has actually received the word that I still have the card. Of course, whoever it is wouldn't just forget about that stash of cocaine. They may be lying low and waiting for me to take it out of my basket. Maybe they figure I'll eventually either throw it away or put it in a drawer or display it on my television like Betsy did.*

Either way, I can't give up now. Until something happens, I need to keep up my efforts to flaunt my card around Happy Haven. I'll have to think of other places in the facility where I might show the card to people who might not know about it or who might not have heard about it. Until I'm positive that everyone here knows about the valentine, I need to keep at it. And I just need to hope that that undercover cop has my back, in case the Happy Haven drug dealer becomes suspicious. She grabbed her walker and headed out for lunch.

Chapter Twenty Six

"Love is like quicksilver in the hand. Leave the fingers open and it stays. Clutch it, and it darts away."

—Dorothy Parker

The chef's Valentine's Day lunch was even more charming than his Valentine's Day breakfast. A tasty tomato soup provided the red. Each soup bowl was set in the middle of a plate which was rimmed with an array of mini heart-shaped sandwiches with various delicate fillings. Essie could hear some of the men at other tables grumbling about the "sissie" food, but the women were on the whole delighted.

"I love Valentine's Day!" proclaimed Marjorie. "You can almost feel the love in the air."

"What I can feel in the air is deodorizer," noted Essie, ever practical, sniffing. "It covers the smell from all the adult diapers."

"Why are you so sour?" asked Opal.

"I'm frustrated because I've been all over Happy Haven, waving this fool valentine I made around, hoping that someone would try to swipe it from me and prove that they're the cocaine dealer," she whispered. "And so far, no one has."

"Essie," said Marjorie in her school teacher voice, "you don't expect the dealer to just come up to you and grab that card, do you? I mean, really. If this person has been able to remain undetected for, who knows, years, they're certainly not going to do anything so ridiculous to jeopardize their set-up."

"You have to learn patience, Essie," added Opal, obviously agreeing with Marjorie. "Surely, the person wants that card back and they're probably trying to figure out a way to get it back. I bet they're quite aware that you have it—or they think you have it. You just need to be patient and watch."

"Opal, what do you think I've been doing all day? Every muscle in my body aches from traipsing all over Happy Haven showing off my card."

"I hope you were cautious in what you said, Essie," said Marjorie, shaking her head.

"Of course," replied Essie. "I put my acting skills to the test. I'm sure I made everyone think I was enamored of this secret admirer person who sent the card and my vanity was motivating me."

"I'm sure no one would ever think that," said Opal, deadpan.

"Well, what would you suggest I do, Opal?" demanded Essie.

"I told you, Essie. You should leave all of this to the police. Let them ferret out this individual. You don't have any idea what you're getting yourself into. If this person discovers what you're up to, that you're working with the police, so to speak, and that you're attempting to set a trap for him, heaven knows how he may retaliate!"

"Indeed, Essie," added Marjorie, "Detective Abbott told us to keep quiet about all of this. He didn't say make a fake valentine and try to catch the culprit by waving it around everywhere!" She shook her little soup spoon at her friend.

The women continued sipping their soup as they spoke in whispered tones, bent over the center of the table. Fay was slumped in her chair, snoring quietly, having downed her soup without a sound while her friends were arguing.

Santos arrived with dessert, a rich chocolate cake topped with raspberries. He set the treats at each woman's place and removed their soup dishes, leaving politely without a comment. Fay evidently smelled the cake and awoke abruptly and dove into the cake with gusto.

"Santos is certainly quiet today," noted Opal.

"Essie probably scared him at breakfast, quizzing him so much about poor Grace Bloom!" suggested Marjorie.

"Oh, birds' turds! I was hardly quizzing him!" responded Essie, licking some chocolate off of her lips. "I merely asked him why he was taking meals to Grace. And, if you recall, he never answered. If that doesn't indicate that something fishy is going on, I don't know what does!"

"Now what could be fishy about Santos taking meals to Grace Bloom in her room, Essie, if indeed that is what he is doing? That seems like a perfectly lovely thing for him to do!" said Opal.

"So why does he have to keep it a secret?" asked Essie.

"Maybe Grace doesn't want anyone to know she's sick," offered Marjorie.

"She's not sick, Marjorie!" cried Essie. "I've seen her at dinner and other people have seen her in the building too!"

"You know," added Opal, "I bumped into Grace during the blood pressure check a few days ago. We actually chatted a bit. She seemed fine to me. Although she didn't stay long. She just got her check and then headed back to her room. She used to come to Quiz Bowl all the time, but I haven't seen her there in quite some time. I mentioned to her that we missed her, but she never said why she hadn't been in a while."

"For heaven's sake, Essie," added Marjorie, "you don't think Grace is the cocaine dealer, do you?"

"No, Marjorie!" snorted Essie. "I don't! But I do think something strange is going on in her room and she and Santos are in on it."

"And they don't want you—or anyone else to know about it!" added Opal. "So honor their wishes!"

"But what if it's something bad?" asked Essie. "Something that threatens Grace? Or Santos? Don't you think we should investigate and find out?"

"Essie," said Opal calmly, "we should not be investigating Grace Bloom or anyone else! And neither should you!"

"You people are too complacent!" replied Essie. "You'd all just stand around while the snake flung apples to Eve in the Garden of Eden!"

"I would, unless the Lord told me to step in and stop it!" retorted Opal.

"The Lord appreciates initiative!" said Essie. "Look at Noah. He built a giant boat and people thought he was nuts but he didn't let them stand in his way. And when the cocaine dealer came knocking and the rain poured down, Noah could say 'I told you so'!"

"Listen, Essie," said Opal with a sigh, leaning back in her chair. "Obviously, I or we can't stop you if you're determined to go ahead with this plan of yours. So, I guess, what I want to say is, I think you're crazy, Essie Cobb, but if you must act like a loon, I will be your backup." She gave Essie a short, forced grimace. "Marjorie?"

"Of course," replied Marjorie. "I'm with you, Essie. But I agree with Opal. You've really gone over the top on this one. Drug dealers are not just nosy neighbors. They have guns. They kill people. I worry about you." She suddenly stuck out her lower lip and a tear dripped down her cheek.

"Oh, scoops of poop!" said Essie. "Marjorie, Opal—and Fay. Are you still awake, Fay?" Fay opened her eyes. "I appreciate all of your support, really I do. But, truly, there's not much you all can do to help. I just have to wait and see if the drug dealer takes the bait I've set for him."

"Well, I for one intend to keep an eye on you," said Opal. "If you don't show up for your meals right on time, you can be assured that I will come looking for you."

"Me too!" added Marjorie.

Fay pointed at herself and nodded.

"Thank you, dear friends," said Essie. "I know you all have my back. And keep your ears open. If you hear or notice anything unusual about the mail, Grace Bloom, Santos delivering meals, anything at all related to these mysteries, please let me know right away."

The women agreed to Essie's requests and having finished their chocolate cake and coffee, wiped their mouths and headed out of the dining hall. Essie rolled herself out, still pondering the issues she had discussed with her friends at lunch.

As far as the fake valentine's card went, she believed that she had shown it to as many people at Happy Haven as she was capable. Obviously, not everyone who lived or worked at Happy Haven had seen it, but surely, the cocaine maven on the premises must now know that Essie still had the card and was no doubt trying to figure out how to get it. He had already attempted to search for it in her apartment without success. Essie guessed that he was thinking that she kept the card with her and if her behavior of this morning was any indication, he would have that belief solidified by now. He probably was trying to figure out a way to get the card from her without her being aware of it. That would mean that he would either have to come into her apartment while she was sleeping and take it from the walker, which would be very risky. Or, he could attempt to sneak it from her walker basket sometime during the day when Essie wasn't aware. Unfortunately, those moments were few and far between, mused Essie. She took her walker with her everywhere she went and the basket in the walker seat was always within a few feet from her at all times. Essie realized that the dealer was probably experiencing a real dilemma.

He probably realized that there were very few opportunities to grab the card from Essie's walker, because of her regular behavior. As Essie contemplated this, she thought that it might be wise to participate in some Happy Haven activities that would allow the dealer greater access to her walker. Hmmm, what activities might those be? Obviously, she didn't intend to actually just leave the walker alone somewhere where the dealer could take the card without Essie knowing. No, she had to find some things she could do where the walker would apparently be left unattended, but where she could still keep her eye on it, surreptitiously.

She stopped at the front desk where Phyllis kept sign-up sheets for various activities going on at Happy Haven throughout the day and for upcoming days. She saw sheets for "grocery trip," "museum field trip," "library trip," and other places outside of the building. These held no interest for her. Also, they wouldn't be appropriate for her plan as it would be unlikely that the drug dealer would follow her on the Happy Haven bus to a field trip.

There were other sheets for in-house activities. She looked these over in an attempt to determine something she could sign up for which would not only announce her presence at a particular location at a particular time (which she reasoned would be advantageous for the dealer), but she was looking for an event or activity which would allow her to be separated from her walker at least for a while. Her eye landed on sign-up sheets for various exercise activities in the building's small gym on the second floor. Essie had been to the little gym a few times, but found it boring. She believed that she got plenty of exercise just rolling around the Happy Haven halls at the breakneck speed she usually went. There was aerobics, dancing, and other high energy-sounding events listed. Essie eventually settled on yoga. She didn't know much about yoga but what she did know was that yoga was a relatively gentle activity without much bouncing and running, something she didn't care for at all. She picked up the attached pencil and signed her name for one of the spots in the yoga class at two o'clock that afternoon. She glanced at her wristwatch. It was past one, so she realized she'd better get going if she was going to clean up and change. She headed back to her room. After her regular bathroom visit, she went into her bedroom and sat on the edge of her bed and attempted to determine which of her various slacks and tops would be appropriate for a yoga class. As Essie had no tights or leotards, which she understood were the *de rigeur* uniform for such a class, she opted for a loose pair of old trousers with elastic around the waist. Over this, she added a very loose knit top that allowed more than her usual amount of movement. It took her almost a half hour to change out of the outfit she had been wearing and pull on this new outfit. She appreciated DeeDee's morning help in dressing even more as she struggled to drag the slacks on over her feet and up her spindly legs without too much damage to her arthritic fingers. Finally, after adding her socks and tennis shoes, she rose and looked at herself in her dresser mirror.

"Yoga, here I come!" she announced.

Chapter Twenty Seven

"Age does not protect you from love. But love, to some extent, protects you from age."

—Jeanne Moreau

Departing the elevator on the second floor, Essie turned in the opposite direction from the arts and crafts room and headed down the opposite hallway which led to the small gym at the other end of Happy Haven. 'Gym' was actually a misnomer. It was not as if they had a basketball court with bleachers. There was only a small, open room with bright lighting. As Essie rolled into the large room that she'd only been in a few times before, the difference in the atmosphere was noticeable.

The room was now dark. Several candles placed on a table near the far end of the room provided the only light. As her eyes adjusted to the dimness, Essie could see that a number of residents had already arrived and had gotten into position for class, or she guessed that's what they were doing. A few women were lying down on the hard floor on some sort of colorful mat. Essie glanced around the room. Near the door, residents had parked their walkers and dropped their canes. She could even see that one woman who used a wheelchair had stationed it near the far side of the room and she had scooted out of her chair and was also lying on the floor on a mat.

The yoga teacher—or yogi—or whatever she was called was visible near the far end, just finishing lighting one of the candles. She was a young woman, her hair in a ponytail.

She was wearing a lavender leotard with white tights. She smiled warmly at residents as they all found a place and unrolled their mats. As she glanced up and saw Essie, she held her hand up in the air as if to say, *just a moment*. She put down her matches on the table and headed over to Essie.

"Greetings," she said softly, her hands together and bowing politely. "Welcome to yoga class. I don't believe we've seen you here before."

"I'm Essie Cobb," replied Essie. "I signed up downstairs."

"Of course," said the yoga instructor. "We're delighted to have you join us, Essie. I'm Nora. If you have any trouble keeping up, please don't be discouraged. Just proceed at your own pace. Remember, the purpose of yoga is for your enlightenment and peace."

And hopefully, to catch a drug dealer, added Essie in her mind.

"You can leave your walker by the door and grab a mat over there," said Nora, pointing to the pile of colorful rubber mats by the entrance. "Just pick a spot and make yourself comfortable. We'll begin in just a moment." Nora bowed again, In that formal Indian manner and Essie nodded, feeling somewhat guilty that she didn't return the appropriate yoga class greeting.

Essie rolled over to where the other residents had parked their walkers and deposited their canes. She pushed hers to a prominent position as close to the entrance as possible. Now how would the drug dealer know this walker was hers?

she thought. So many of the walkers looked alike. Of course, she always recognized her walker, but then she never was really parted from it. Giving her basket seat a little good luck pat, she carefully inched over to the group of residents already on their mats near the far end. Her bones creaked as she lowered herself to the floor and unrolled her pink mat. Once flattened, the mat had a squeaky, bouncy quality. Essie crawled cautiously onto the mat and smiled at the residents nearby.

"Welcome to yoga," whispered one lady on her right, her right leg up in the air. Essie wondered if the leg raised perpendicular to the floor was the traditional yoga greeting. She attempted to force her leg into the air, but she was able to extend it only as far as her knee.

"That's as far as that one will go," she noted. "Maybe the other one has more stretch." She put the first leg on the floor and attempted to raise the other leg to no avail. Plopping the leg back onto the mat, she lay there exhausted from this minimal physical exercise.

"And class hasn't even begun," she said to herself.

At that moment, Nora came away from the candles and out to the front of the group. She performed a deep bow, the top part of her body remaining clutched to the lower half for a painfully long period of time. At least, that's how Essie viewed it.

"Greetings, students," Nora said in a gentle, almost inaudible voice. "Are we ready to begin?" The residents nodded and some made sounds of agreement. Nora then began by announcing various positions. The first seemed relatively simple to Essie. At least, at first. Nora demonstrated. She lay face down on her mat and pushed upwards with her hands, looking at the ceiling. She then seemed to hold that pose as if she were frozen. The residents—most of whom seemed to be regular attendees—repeated Nora's pose, although none of them looked as lovely and relaxed as Nora did. Most of the residents had looks of pain and torture on their faces.

Essie rolled over with difficulty until she was on her stomach. *How hard can this be?* she wondered. She pushed her body upwards with her hands, looking at the ceiling, but glancing down at Nora at the front of the group to see if she was capturing the pose correctly. It seemed to be right. So why did it feel so uncomfortable? Surely, no one could remain like this for long, and yet when she glanced around the room, most the residents were holding Nora's pose. *Egad, Chad!* moaned Essie to herself. There's just too much of me to hold up like this for this long. She could feel her elbows starting to sway back and forth. *Please, don't buckle!* she urged them. She clenched her teeth in an attempt to maintain the pose that everyone else appeared to be holding smoothly. All of a sudden, she collapsed and her chin hit the pink mat with a thud.

"Don't be upset if you cannot hold the pose for long," droned Nora as if she wasn't referring at all to the fact that Essie had just plopped noisily onto her mat. "It's the effort not the time that counts." Essie panted on her mat in a prone position, her face to one side. Finally, she rolled over onto her back and sat up while she waited for the group to conclude the pose. *Now, how could that woman talk and hold that pose at the same time?* thought Essie. *It was all I could do to keep my head above my shoulders for more than two seconds. I thought yoga was supposed to be relaxing. Ha!*

Eventually, Nora gently pulled out of the pose and the other residents followed.

"Now, for our second position," said the yoga leader. She stood up on her mat and bent down and touched her toes. The class followed her actions. Then gradually she walked her hands forward and away from her feet until they were at least several feet in front of her. When she had reached the correct location, she appeared to freeze in place. The residents followed her, although Essie detected quite a number of grunts and groans along the way, particularly as they reached down for their toes.

Essie hadn't stood up and touched her toes since—well, she couldn't remember ever standing up and reaching down to touch her toes. She couldn't think of a practical reason to do such a thing. Now, obviously, there was a reason. Slowly she bent her body, dropping her hands lower and lower towards the mat. She could see the floor in the distance, but she couldn't quite reach it. She realized that she couldn't even begin this second pose until she was able to touch her toes. She bounced up and down, figuring she might give herself a little push, but her hands refused to hit the floor. She continued this procedure over and over. The other residents had all been able to reach the floor and had moved their hands out to form the little triangle that was created by this body position. Nora spoke soothingly to encourage the class. At one point, Nora calmly stood from her pose and moved to Essie. She whispered in her ear.

"Don't feel you have to reach your toes, Essie. You can aim for further out in front. Here, let me help you." Nora grabbed Essie's waist and held tight as she directed Essie to reach out. Essie stretched her arms out and Nora gradually lowered Essie's body until Essie's hands were on the floor about three feet in front of her feet. "There you go. Now just hold this position as long as you can."

Easy for you to say, Essie wanted to snap back at the sweet-natured yoga teacher. Essie now found herself in an uncomfortable position that she had no idea how to extricate herself from. If she moved a hand, her entire body would plummet to the ground. She seriously thought she might break a bone if she so much as moved a finger. Nora came around again.

"Let's bring you up, Essie," she said. She pulled up on Essie's waist again and Essie suddenly was upright. *Forces of horses!* she thought. *This little woman has a lot of strength.*

After these opening poses, Nora had the class lie down on their mats. As she lay on her plastic mat with her legs stretched at an odd angle, Essie felt as if there would be no way her poor leg would ever return to its normal position. She'd probably need orthopedic surgery. When her classmates carefully extricated their legs from their poses and put their feet back on the floor, Essie realized that her feet were permanently stuck in this position. She probably looked like a human pretzel. She'd be ready to join the circus once she graduated from this class.

Lovely Nora appeared as if from a cloud and amazingly performed her magic again. With a quick pull on Essie's feet, Essie suddenly found her body in one piece and herself lying in a prone position on her back, panting as if she'd just run a marathon. The instructor smiled sweetly and returned to the front of the class.

Finally, after a few more of what she referred to as "simple" positions, Nora announced that class was finished. She rose and calmly bowed to the class. The class returned her gesture and then rolled up their plastic mats and placed them back in a pile by the door where they came in. Some of the residents remained, chatting with one another. Nora disappeared as ethereally as she had come. Essie had not seen her in the building before. She assumed that Nora was an instructor who came in from the outside to conduct these classes and not one of the regular staff members at Happy Haven.

Essie hobbled over as best she could to where the walkers were parked. She found her walker and realized that she had not looked up even once throughout the entire class to see if anyone was disturbing her walker while she was doing yoga. She quickly but discreetly opened the seat cover and glanced inside. The cream-colored envelope remained on top. She lifted it up and looked inside; the homemade fake valentine she had concocted was still there. Apparently, the dealer had not used this opportunity to steal it from her. She would have to figure out another way to entice him to come looking for it.

As she rolled out the gym door and towards the elevator, she felt every muscle in her body. And this was not a good thing. Some parts of her body she never wanted to feel. So much for yoga being a gentle activity. *Could all that weird yoga stuff really be beneficial*? she wondered.   Certainly, she'd never need to use any of those weird poses to do anything. None that she could think of anyway.

The elevator door was open for which she was grateful. The cab was crowded with people. As she glanced at her watch, she realized she had plenty of time before dinner. After all that activity, she'd surely need a nap.

Chapter Twenty Eight

"One word frees us of all the weight and pain of life. That word is love."

—Sophocles

When she exited the elevator on the first floor, she could tell there was something going on. The number of people gathered in the family room was far greater than normal. The noise level was much higher too. As she pushed and shoved her walker through the massive crowd of people, many of whom were not Happy Haven residents, and rounded the corner into the main lobby, it dawned on her what all the commotion was about. This was the crowd that had gathered for that Dr. Love, the authority on the history of romance.

Essie wanted nothing more than to make a beeline for her room and take a nap. Every muscle in her ninety-year-old body had made itself known during the yoga workout. *Ouch*, she cried out loud as a man bumped into her and almost knocked her down. She pushed ahead and could see the cause of the excitement.

Standing at the fireplace was a tall, dark-haired man of movie-star good looks. He had exquisite posture and just a touch of grey at his temples. His beautifully tailored suit was probably made in Italy, Essie surmised. It fit every curve of his body to perfection. Now if this man were her secret admirer, she might actually consider giving him a tumble. Sue Barber was standing next to him, apparently waiting for the starting time. Essie glanced at her watch. It was a few minutes before two.

As she stood frozen, staring at the guest speaker, she heard her name called out. Looking up, she spied Marjorie, Opal, and Fay—all seated together on one of the long sofas near the fireplace. Marjorie was patting the seat between herself and Opal and motioning for Essie to sit there.

Nefertiti's nipples! she mumbled to herself. *There goes my nap!* She maneuvered her walker through the buzzing crowd over to the sofa where her friends were seated.

"Come on, Essie!" cried Marjorie. "Sit here with us!"

"Put your walker by the wall," ordered Opal. Essie looked over to a nearby wall where her pals and several other residents had parked their vehicles. Essie was too tired to argue so she nudged her walker among the others and limped over the few feet to the sofa and plopped down between Marjorie and Opal. Opal had the end seat and Fay was beside her in her wheelchair.

"Quickly, everyone!" shouted Sue Barber. "Take your places. We're about ready to begin."

Essie could see a local news team positioned near the front entrance. A woman was holding a microphone and she was accompanied by a young man holding a large video camera.

"So this is a big event?" Essie asked her friends.

"We may be on television!" said Marjorie, fluffing her hair and peering over her shoulder at the camera behind them. From another location, a camera flashed.   Phyllis and Violet stood watch over the entire event from the front desk. Some of the kitchen workers had even stopped preparing for the next meal and were standing in the doorway of the dining hall, some even with a dish towel or pan in their hands.

"I told you Dr. Love was a big deal, Essie," explained Opal. "Where were you, anyway?"

"Yoga," said Essie with a deep sigh.

"Yoga?" asked Marjorie. "What would possess you to go there?"

"That's what I'm asking myself," replied Essie. "I have a new appreciation for contortionists."

"Okay, residents and guests!" announced Sue Barber, using her loud stage voice. "Happy Haven is delighted to have with us today a world famous expert on love and romance. And how appropriate is that! Being it's Valentine's Day!"

The crowd tittered appropriately and the attractive guest speaker smiled benignly.

"Our speaker is Dr. Emmett Flynn—otherwise known as Dr. Love. He is the head of Grace College's Anthropology Department and is an expert on the history of romantic love. Dr. Flynn speaks all over the world on this topic and we are especially lucky today that he is able to stop by Happy Haven to regale us with some of his fascinating research. He even tells me that he is happy to answer specific questions about love and romance from audience members. So, residents, if you have any love problems, here's the guy who can provide the solution!"

The man chuckled humbly at this last description as Sue Barber held out her hand for him to take over.

"I was going to say 'ladies and gentlemen,'" began Dr. Love, his chiseled features making him look almost like a fabled Roman statue. "However, it appears there are far more ladies here than men!"

The women all laughed.

"Truthfully," said Dr. Love in a confidential tone, "I prefer it that way." With that, all the women in the audience produced audible sighs. From this intimate beginning, Dr. Love continued to weave a spell over the large crowd that was jammed into the lobby, with quite a bit of overflow in the family room. He used stories from history and from his own research to explain how various romantic practices and terms had come to be. Every once in a while, he would suggest that people today experienced similar things and ask the audience if any of them had any examples to share. The residents were quick to open up to the gregarious speaker and soon began sharing their own personal romantic stories. Essie was entranced. At one point, Dr. Love began discussing the giving and receiving of valentines and this elicited several residents to offer examples of interesting valentines they had received over the years. Dr. Love then mentioned the history and development of the concept of the 'secret admirer' and Dave Esperti, from somewhere in the family room, shouted out.

"Have Essie Cobb tell about her secret admirer, Doc!" yelled Dave.

Oh, no, thought Essie, scrunching down in the sofa in an attempt to hide between Marjorie and Opal.

"A secret admirer?" asked Dr. Love, looking around. His piercing blue eyes captured Essie, now in a little mound on the sofa. "Would that be you, Miss?" he asked in a voice dripping with intimacy as he tipped his head of thick hair in Essie's direction.

Essie's attempt to disappear was to no avail. Marjorie and Opal both punched her in the ribs.

"This is Essie, Dr. Love," yelled Marjorie, pointing at her friend.

"She has a secret admirer," added Opal, nodding and smiling idiotically at the speaker. Essie had never seen Opal behave like a school girl before, yet here she was acting like a love-struck teenager.

"So," declared Dr. Love, reaching out his hand and grabbing Essie's hand, and almost effortlessly lifting her from the depths of the sofa and bringing her up to the front of the crowd with him. "So, you are the lady who has a secret admirer?" He was holding both of Essie's hands tightly now and looking straight into her eyes. Essie could smell his after shave and it smelled really good. A manly odor. This man not only knew a lot about romance, he obviously also put what he knew into practice.

"Uh, yes," she mumbled as several cameras flashed. Apparently, a photograph of Dr. Love holding hands with a female was far more interesting than one of him just talking. Even if the female was ninety years old.

"So, Miss Essie," Dr. Love said to Essie, and loud enough for the entire group to hear. "What do you know about this admirer? Do you have any ideas who it might be?"

"No," replied Essie. This sad response brought about a collective sigh.

"You mean," continued Dr. Love, "you don't think it's one of these fine gentlemen..." he said and gestured to some of the men in the audience.

"I don't think so," replied Essie. "It came from Boston." The crowd laughed.

"Maybe it's Paul Revere," suggested Dr. Love gallantly.

"I'm old, Dr. Love, but I'm not that old," snorted Essie. The crowd laughed and more cameras flashed.

"Well, Miss Essie," said Dr. Love, "I hope you figure out who your admirer is, but if you don't, just remember that the concept of the secret admirer is truly one of the most romantic in all the history of love. Someone who loves but who doesn't expect to ever have this love reciprocated. Now, that's truly special. Don't you think?" He spread his free hand as he described the phenomenon of the secret admirer to the audience, all the while clasping Essie's hands with his other hand. Essie considered his ideas. Of course, she knew it was all rubbish, but he had a nice chin and he smelled really good.

Eventually, Dr. Love assisted Essie back to her seat and concluded his presentation. Sue Barber jumped up and thanked him profusely for his entertaining talk and the crowd agreed by applauding loudly for a long time. After the speech, Dr. Love continued to speak informally with Sue and several of the reporters came forward and asked to take close-ups. One cameraman wanted a repeat photo of Dr. Love holding Essie's hands, so she obliged more than willingly by posing again. Marjorie, Opal, and Fay seemed to enjoy all of this vicariously from their seats on the sofa. Finally, Dr. Love made his exit and residents and guests dispersed.

"Essie," said Marjorie excitedly, "you're a star!"

"They'll probably put your picture in the newspaper," added Opal. The four women now found themselves almost alone in the deserted lobby.

"What good will that do me?" asked Essie. "Will it help me identify my admirer?"

"Quiet, Essie," said Marjorie.

"That's not what you were saying a bit ago, Marjorie!" said Essie. "You were more than willing to volunteer me as the recipient of a secret admirer card for Dr. Love."

"And you loved every minute of it," noted Marjorie.

"It's true, Essie," added Opal. "You practically fainted when that man took your hand and raised it to his lips."

"Well, he smelled good," said Essie.

"I smell good," offered Opal, "but you don't faint when I touch you."

"Never mind, Opal," sneered Essie. "You're making too much of this."

"Besides," countered Opal. "I wasn't the one who volunteered you. It was Dave Esperti, if I remember correctly."

"Yes, Essie," added Marjorie, "Dave seems to have a bit of a crush on you."

"As does Hubert Darby," said Opal.

"And a secret admirer—fake or not! How come you have all the boyfriends, Essie?" asked Marjorie.

"Probably because I don't want any boyfriends," said Essie, scowling. "This conversation is exhausting. I have work to do."

"You mean like a nap?" asked Opal.

"You try yoga, Opal, and I bet you'll want a nap too!" snapped Essie. At that moment, Santos passed through the lobby and headed towards her hallway carrying a food tray. "See you all later," she said cheerily. She pushed herself up, wobbly from the soft sofa, and limped uncomfortably over to the far wall where she had parked her walker. She grabbed the handles and backed it out of the group of other vehicles. She headed off through the family room, following close on Santos's heels.

At the end of the corridor, she hung back, peeking around the corner. As she looked down the hallway, she saw Santos stop at Grace Bloom's doorway and knock. The door opened promptly and Santos entered.

"Root beer floats!" she cried to herself. "That does it!" She pushed her walker around the corner and down the hall to

Grace Bloom's doorway. Without hesitation, she knocked.
She knocked a second time. She could hear people inside
mumbling. Finally, Grace opened the door a crack and
peeked out.

"Essie!" she cried, obviously surprised. "What do you
want?"

"I want Santos," said Essie. "I saw him come in here with a
food tray. I assumed it was because you are sick, Grace.
But you don't look sick to me!"

Chapter Twenty Nine

"There's a lot to be said for self-delusionment when it comes to matters of the heart."

—Diane Frolov and Andrew Schneider

Grace appeared mystified and remained clutching the door frame, staring at Essie. Finally, Essie saw Santos's head pop up over Grace's.

"Miss Essie!" he whispered. "What are you doing here?"

"I might ask the same of you, Santos!" said Essie, pointing her finger. "You told me you weren't bringing trays to Grace. You obviously lied."

"This doesn't concern you, Miss Essie," Santos whispered.

Grace shrugged her shoulders and looked up at the young man. "Oh, for heaven's sake," she sighed. "We might as well let her in. She's going to pester us until we do." Santos gave Grace a pained and quizzical look. Eventually, he relented and the door was opened. Santos and Grace stood aside and allowed Essie to enter Grace's small apartment. This living room was almost identical to Essie's. Of course, Grace had different furniture, but Essie knew exactly where the bedroom and bathroom were located because the floor plan was the same as hers. Nothing about Grace's homey apartment would indicate that she was ill. Essie saw no signs of medicine or piles of tissues or anything medical. Grace was dressed and showed no obvious signs of distress. She didn't even see the food tray that Santos had brought.

It was neither in Grace's small kitchen nor anywhere visible in her living room.

"So?" asked Essie. "What's all the secrecy? Why are you bringing Grace a food tray? Are you sick, Grace? I'm just concerned."

"Sometimes, Essie," said Grace, hands on hips, "sometimes it's best to stay out of other people's business." She shook her head in annoyance.

"I am sure Miss Essie will keep secret, Miss Bloom," said Santos to Grace.

"What secret?" asked Essie.

"Oh, Lord!" sighed Grace. "Come on! I'll show you!" She motioned for Essie to follow her into the bedroom. Santos followed the two women. Arriving in the bedroom, Essie saw immediately what Santos and Grace had been working so hard to keep secret. On one side of the room was Grace's small bed, flush against the wall. On the other side, on the floor, a large blanket was spread out, surrounded by a wall of pillows. Inside the pillows, flailing around were six or seven rambunctious little white and black puppies of an indeterminate breed. They were all making sad, whiny noises. A small doll's bottle full of milk resided on Grace's nightstand. The food tray that Santos had apparently delivered was on Grace's bed. Instead of a plate of food, it held a paper carton of milk.

"Puppies!" cried Essie. "That's your big secret?"

"Obviously," said Grace, "I can't let the staff know. Pets are not allowed at Happy Haven. You know that, Essie."

Essie did know this restriction and although sometimes Happy Haven made exceptions to this rule, such as when a resident required a companion dog, residents were not allowed to bring in pets merely for social purposes.

"How many are there?" asked Essie.

"Six," said Grace. "The mother is dead. My grandson found the puppies behind his home. He wanted to keep them and care for them himself, but his parents..."

"Grandson beg Miss Bloom to take puppies," added Santos. "She very good mother to puppies." He smiled at Essie. "You understand, Miss Essie. You understand about taking care of babies." And, of course, Essie did understand. She had been a mother—never of dogs before—but she could certainly understand Grace Bloom's determination not to see these little creatures abandoned after having lost their mother.

"My husband would have insisted on taking them in when he was alive," added Grace. "He was a vet and he would have taken these puppies in without a second thought. I couldn't do otherwise. Santos has been helping me by bringing me milk for them and by babysitting them so I could get out to my meals and other things from time to time. He's also found new homes for most of them when they are old enough."

"Yes, Santos is good about that," added Essie. "Well, don't worry, Grace. Your secret is safe with me. I'm surely not going to tell anyone. And, if you need some help babysitting these little fellows, just let me know. I have a bit of experience in that area myself." She smiled warmly at the two human puppy parents and they returned her smile. Essie knelt down, her knees creaking audibly, and rubbed the nose of one of the pups. The little dog responded by licking Essie's hand madly and whimpering.

Eventually, after everyone had made peace with each other, Essie left Grace Bloom's apartment and rolled herself back down the corridor to her own place. When she arrived, she flung herself into her recliner, moaning painfully from all of her recent activities. She started to drift off, but before she allowed herself to sleep, she reached over to her walker just to check on the envelope in her basket. She realized that she hadn't looked at it since yoga class, and she felt the need to double check to make sure it was still there. When she raised the black seat lid, she gasped. The cream-colored envelope was not in its usual spot on the top of the pile of objects. She rummaged through her belongings in the basket. Maybe the card had fallen down the side and slipped to the bottom of the pile. She brought out everything from the basket and carefully sifted through every item. No. The fake valentine was missing. There was no doubt. She had not misplaced it. Someone had taken it between the time she had left yoga and the time she returned from Grace Bloom's apartment. She reviewed where she had been and considered the most logical time and place for the drug dealer to have absconded with the valentine.

The obvious answer was during Dr. Love's speech. Essie had left her walker near the wall with all the other walkers. She had sat on the sofa with her friends during the presentation. There were so many people milling about during Dr. Love's speech. She also had to admit that she wasn't really paying very close attention to her walker during the speech. Anyone could have passed by the walkers by the wall and surreptitiously lifted the seat and discreetly lifted out her fake valentine. It was on the top. It would be easy to steal. Even so, Essie wasn't panicked. She realized that what she had expected to happen, what she had hoped would happen, had happened. The dealer had struck. Now she hoped that her plan would work and that the Happy Haven drug dealer would fall victim to it and would soon be exposed. She knew, however, that time was of the essence. Even though she hadn't informed Detective Abbott of her plan in advance, now that the card was gone, she believed that she needed to let him know—both because it would soon be likely that he would be able to arrest the dealer, and if anything should go wrong when the dealer discovered the surprise that Essie had planted inside the little heart and the dealer responded with anger or violence, the police would be there to protect the residents, including Essie.

She reached for her telephone and got out the business card that Detective Abbott had given her from her basket. She dialed Abbott's private number. The man answered promptly and Essie explained her situation. Abbott was shocked and not terribly thrilled that Essie had implemented this plot to catch the drug dealer on her own, but even so, he informed Essie that he and his officers would be over to Happy Haven immediately. He told her to stay put. Essie assumed he meant for her to stay in her room. Of course, Essie had no intention of doing that. She wanted to be somewhere where she could see if and when the dealer revealed himself. She believed it would be sooner rather than later. Surely, now that the dealer had the card in his possession, it wouldn't be long before he tried to open the little fake heart and remove what he assumed would be his supply of cocaine. What a surprise was awaiting him!

Essie put her exhaustion on the back burner and agonizingly dragged herself out of her recliner. Grabbing her trusty walker, which she thought of warmly now as her virtual partner in crime detection, she headed out to the lobby.

Amazingly enough, the lobby that had so recently been filled with people was now almost completely empty. Only a few residents sat in front of the fireplace. One man was reading a newspaper as he enjoyed the warmth. Another lady appeared to be waiting for someone. She had on her coat and hat and was looking towards the front entrance. Essie carefully chose a high-backed chair in a corner where she could view most of the entire lobby without too many people seeing her.

Phyllis stood at the front desk talking on the phone. A few kitchen workers moved around in the dining hall. Essie could see them through the glass walls setting up tables for dinner. Violet Hendrickson entered quickly from her office near the main entrance. She appeared agitated. She headed over to Phyllis who quickly hung up the phone when she saw the Happy Haven director coming towards her in an annoyed state. Essie observed their heated discussion from afar. Violet was showing Phyllis her hands. She rubbed her hands together and pointed at them. Phyllis looked startled and uncomfortable. She held up her hand for Violet to wait at the desk and she headed into the little back room behind the counter. Violet scowled and looked around in obvious annoyance. Essie tried to see Violet's hands to see what was upsetting her about them, but Violet had her palms placed flat down on the counter. Soon, Phyllis returned with a bottle of a clear liquid and some cotton balls. Violet grabbed the items with nary a thank you to Phyllis and stormed off into her office.

Now, I wonder what sort of substance Violet got on her hands? thought Essie. *Could it be ink? If so, I wonder where she got it from?* Essie smiled to herself. Was this little mystery coming to a close?

At that moment, Detective Abbott entered the main entrance. He was followed by Chavez and Magee. Phyllis looked shocked to see the two police officers. Abbott came over to Phyllis and spoke to her. Chavez and Magee stood behind him, looking authoritative. Abbott looked around and his eyes fell on Essie sitting in the far corner. He motioned for Chavez and Magee to remain at the main entrance which they did, stationing themselves on either side of the doorway. Abbott wandered over to Essie, and calmly took a seat on the brick fireplace edge next to her chair.

"So, Miss Essie," he said. "You're out to catch this crook on your own, are you?" He shook his head patronizingly.

"Yes, Detective," replied Essie, "and I believe I have succeeded."

"Oh?" asked Abbott. "You mean you caught this crook? Where is he?" Abbott looked around skeptically. He crossed his arms and smiled at Essie.

Essie explained her fake valentine and how she had set it to trap the dealer. She told Abbott how she had shown the card all over Happy Haven in hopes of attracting the culprit to try to swipe it. When she found the card missing, she realized that the dealer had indeed taken the card, so she came down to see if the dealer would show himself.

"Show himself?" asked Abbott.

"Yes, Detective," replied Essie. "If anyone opened that card I made, then went further and cut open the little heart I made—and nobody but the drug dealer would have any reason to do that—then they'd find themselves with their hands covered with indelible ink. I believe you'll discover that there is one member of our staff who now has very black palms."

"Who?" asked Abbott.

"Violet Hendrickson," said Essie. "The Director of Happy Haven. She just retreated to her office with some sort of cleaner. I believe she's trying to remove the ink from her hands."

"Miss Essie," said Abbott firmly. "Wait here." He motioned to Chavez and Magee to follow him and the three police officers headed back down the office hallway next to the main entrance.

Essie remained in her chair in the lobby for what seemed a very long time. Eventually, however, Abbott returned from the office hallway followed by Chavez and Magee who were escorting Violet Hendrickson between them. Violet was handcuffed and she was staring down at the floor. Her face was red and tear-stained. Essie almost felt sorry for her—but not quite. Abbott motioned Chavez and Magee to take Violet away. Phyllis witnessed this whole event silently, her mouth wide open the entire time. The other residents also looked on, apparently stunned as the Happy Haven director was arrested and taken away in police custody.

Abbott stood for a moment at the counter, apparently explaining things to Phyllis. Then he stepped back over to where Essie was sitting.

"You are some lady, Miss Essie," said Abbott with a long whistle. "I don't suppose you'd like a job on the narcotics task force, would you?"

"No, thank you, Detective," replied Essie. "My life is exciting enough."

Chapter Thirty

"Love is, above all else, the gift of oneself."

—Jean Anouilh

Valentine's Day was a distant memory. All of the fancy decorations had been removed. In fact, the staff had actually started to hang shamrocks in preparation for St. Patrick's Day. Most of the residents had forgotten all of the excitement of Dr. Love's speech and the media coverage of their little assisted living facility. A few had even forgotten the shock of having Violet Hendrickson, the Happy Haven director, arrested and accused of dealing illegal drugs.

Even so, there were quite a few residents and staff members gathered in the lobby that morning for a ceremony that also drew some local media—although not quite as much attention as the aforementioned Dr. Love. One lone reporter with a camera stood in the lobby by the fireplace awaiting the opportunity to snap a candid shot. Essie's family—Pru, Kurt, and Claudia—and their spouses and children all stood together to one side, obviously amazed and proud of their mother and grandmother. Mindy, who had had a small part in Essie's recent adventure, was visibly the most proud. Indeed, before the ceremony, Essie had shown Mindy the fake valentine she had made that had lured Violet into confessing. Abbott had returned the card to Essie for her scrapbook—minus the ink-filled heart.

Detective Abbott stood in the center of the room, attired in his finest dress uniform. Chavez and Magee stood nearby, also neatly uniformed. Essie stood behind her walker, next to Abbott.

"Miss Cobb," said Abbott, in a deep baritone voice, "the Reardon Police Department wishes to present you with this official letter of commendation for your assistance in the identification and capture of Violet Hendrickson, alias Viola Dunlap, alias Viviane Dugan, on charges of illegal drug dealing." Abbott held up a certificate framed in a gold case. He held it out towards Essie and she placed her hands on the frame. The reporter lifted his camera and snapped away. Essie and Abbott smiled and froze their poses.

Abbott continued speaking to the gathered crowd, "The Reardon Police Department wishes you, the residents of Happy Haven, to know how much we admire and appreciate the efforts of Miss Cobb. Although we don't condone Miss Cobb's singular heroics and daring, we do certainly appreciate her efforts, which we all consider above and beyond the call of duty."

The small group of staff and residents applauded.

"In truth," continued Abbott, speaking now more informally, "we don't quite know what to make of Essie Cobb. It's not every day that a ninety-year-old woman foils a huge drug ring like this one all alone."

"Oh, but Detective," interjected Essie, "I had a lot of help from my friends Marjorie, Opal, and Fay!" She smiled and pointed to her pals sitting attentively all together on the sofa near the fireplace. The three women all turned and waved at the crowd, particularly the photographer. "And, of course, Betsy Rollingford helped too. She got a secret admirer card last year. If it weren't for Betsy I never would have realized that Violet was using all of the residents to bring drugs into Happy Haven." Essie waved at Betsy who was sitting in the middle of the lobby. Betsy rose and took a tiny bow much to the delight of all the residents.

"Yes, of course," said Abbott. "You obviously had a lot of help, Miss Essie. But, still it was your plan. And it's hard to believe that a lady of your...uh...experience...could accomplish such a feat!"

"It's not hard for us to believe," said Dave Esperti, standing in the rear. "We've all known Essie was a pistol for a long time!" The group laughed.

"A pistol she is," agreed Abbott, turning to Chavez and Magee and smiling at them. The two officers returned the glance. "Anyway, for the record, the suspect who Essie helped us arrest pleaded guilty in circuit court yesterday. We have her confession and the DA has arranged a plea deal with Miss Hendrickson in exchange for her testimony on the larger national drug ring of which she was a part. We are happy to say that because of this, the Boston Police have been able to put a crime syndicate out of business."

"All because of Essie!" declared a man near the back. Essie thought it was the man who'd harassed her in arts and crafts class.

"Yes, because of Essie," agreed Abbott. "It's true and it's sad that this arrest takes away Happy Haven's director."

"It's not sad to me!" declared Essie, stomping her foot. The crowd roared.

"But, I'm sure Happy Haven will be able to replace Miss Hendrickson with a fine new director quite soon."

"Make sure they do a better background check," yelled out a resident from the back.

"In the meantime," continued Abbott, "know that the Reardon Police Department will be here for you if you need us! I believe I can safely speak for my fellow officers when I say that this facility will always hold a special place in our hearts."   He glanced over at Magee and Chavez who were beaming. Chavez rubbed a tear from her eye with the sleeve of her uniform jacket.

Essie looked around. She didn't see Santos or Grace Bloom, so she figured they were both busy feeding puppies. Phyllis stood at the front desk in her usual spot. Essie wondered how she would fare without Violet Hendrickson; Phyllis had always seemed so attached to Violet. But as she looked at Phyllis, the desk clerk was smiling warmly at Essie. Maybe the transition to a new director of Happy Haven wouldn't be as hard as she imagined.

Eventually, Detective Abbott finished his glowing comments about Essie and the commendation ceremony ended with the group slowly migrating to the dining hall where cookies and punch were served to all. Essie's children remained in the lobby to meet the three policemen and to hear them describe personally how they'd first met Essie and how her concern over the white powder in her secret admirer valentine eventually led to solving this major crime. All three of the police officers appeared to be enjoying talking about Essie and her exploits. Essie's children seemed a bit overwhelmed that Essie had done what she had done all by herself. There was a lot of polite smiling, but Essie knew that eventually she was probably going to be lectured by one or more of her children about taking unnecessary risks.

One person who wouldn't lecture her was her granddaughter Mindy. As her children and grandchildren stood around talking to the three police officers, Essie drew Mindy aside. She wanted to get this young woman's take on the recent events.

"Grandma!" declared Mindy, giving Essie a warm hug, "you are my hero! Not only do you catch a criminal, but you do it by using your very clever art skills!"

"I just used what stuff I had on hand," said Essie, downplaying her efforts. She knew quite honestly that a thorough investigation of her fake valentine would quickly indicate that it came nowhere near the quality of the one sent by her secret admirer in Boston.

"Even so," said Mindy. "I bet none of my friends' grandmas could ever do anything like this!"

"Well, you taught me about the artistic features of the card, Mindy," said Essie. She felt a deep empathy for this young woman who always seemed so shy and socially awkward.

"I'm glad I could help you, Grandma," replied Mindy. "If you ever need help on any of your adventures, you can always ask me!"

"I will keep that in mind, my dear," replied Essie. "Now, how about some punch and cookies?" Mindy smiled and the two women headed for the dining hall, along with the crowd of well-wishers.

As Essie stood in the dining hall, nibbling cookies and sipping punch, surrounded by her friends and family, she felt a tap on her elbow.

"Essie," said Hubert Darby softly. "I just wanted you to know how much I admire you." He blushed and rocked back and forth on his squeaky shoes.

"Thank you, Hubert," replied Essie. "Truth be told, I liked your valentine the best."

Hubert's face turned red and he gasped for breath, pulling and twisting his suspenders nervously. Then, suddenly, he bent over and planted a kiss on Essie's cheek. Essie froze and smiled. Everyone gathered in the dining hall turned and looked at the large, befuddled man who was smooching the guest of honor.

"Happy Valentine's Day, Miss Essie!" said Hubert. Essie, for maybe the first time in her life, was speechless. Everyone cheered and Hubert and Essie smiled warmly at each other.

ABOUT THE AUTHOR

VALENTINED is the third in Patricia Rockwell's Essie Cobb senior sleuth mysteries. The other books are BINGOED and PAPOOSED. Ms. Rockwell also writes the Pamela Barnes acoustic mystery series which includes SOUNDS OF MURDER, FM FOR MURDER, VOICE MAIL MURDER, and STUMP SPEECH MURDER.

Ms. Rockwell has spent most of her adult life teaching. Her Bachelors' and Masters' degrees are from the University of Nebraska in Speech, and her Ph.D. is from the University of Arizona in Communication. She was on the faculty at the University of Louisiana at Lafayette for thirteen years, retiring in 2007. Her publications are extensive, with over 20 peer-reviewed articles in scholarly journals, several textbooks, and a research volume published by Edwin Mellen Press. In addition, she served for eight years as editor of the *Louisiana Communication Journal*. Her research focuses primarily on deception, sarcasm, and vocal cues. Dr. Rockwell is presently living in Aurora, Illinois, with her husband Milt, also a retired educator. The couple has two adult children.